SACRED TALONS

Writing about people and subjects he encountered in close quarters, **AA. MADHAVAN** set all his stories in and around the Chaalai Bazaar, where he lived all his life and ran his father's utensils shop. Taking literary naturalism a step ahead, he wrote with such detachment that his works were devoid of authorial intervention or philosophizing. His works largely dealt with subjects like morbidity, sexuality and human vulnerability without any shade of moralizing. Also a translator of several Malayalam books into Tamil, Aa. Madhavan won the Kendra Sahitya Akademi Award in 2015 for his collected prose writings titled *Ilakkiya Chuvadugal*.

RAMAKRISHNAN V. is a literature graduate with experience in translation and creative writing. His translation of five short stories, including those written by Imayam, Ravikumar and Abimani, appeared in a Dalit short story anthology titled *In Defiance: Our Stories* which was unveiled in the Chennai Book Fair, 2022. He has also translated a collection of short stories by Arignar Anna, the former Tamil Nadu chief minister, under the title *Help Me with This Tricky Case* (2023). He has completed his PhD in English literature, on popular culture, at the University of Madras. A part of his research focuses on the dynamics of translation in popular culture.

MISSION STATEMENT

This is an initiative of the Tamil Nadu Textbook and Educational Services Corporation (TNTB & ESC) under the aegis of one of the announcements for the year 2021–22, titled 'Thisaidhorum Dravidam' by Honourable Minister for School Education Thiru. Anbil Mahesh Poyyamozhi to identify and translate into English, Kannada, Malayalam and Telugu, Tamil literary works, that they might enhance the reach of Tamil antiquity, tradition and contemporaneity and enrich World literature and to also translate significant literary voices from other Dravidian languages into Tamil. Both ventures are to be undertaken as either independent or joint publications with collaborating publishers.

Members, Academic Advisory Committee (Translation)

1. Dr. R. Balakrishnan, IAS, Researcher and Writer
2. Thiru. S. Ramakrishnan, Writer
3. Thiru. S. Madasamy, Educationist

Project Execution Team

1. Thiru. Dindigul I. Leoni, Chairperson, TNTB & ESC
2. Dr. M. Aarthi, IAS, Managing Director, TNTB & ESC
3. Dr. C. Usha Rani, Member Secretary, TNTB & ESC
4. Dr. T.S. Saravanan, Honorary Advisor, TNTB & ESC
5. Dr. P. Saravanan, Assistant Director (Publications), TNTB & ESC
6. Ms S. Thenmozhi, Deputy Director, TNTB & ESC
7. Thiru. M. Appanasamy, Consultant, TNTB & ESC
8. Tmt. Mini Krishnan, Co-ordinating Editor, TNTB & ESC

SACRED TALONS

AA. MADHAVAN

TRANSLATED FROM THE TAMIL BY
RAMAKRISHNAN V.

hachette INDIA

First published in Tamil in 1980 by Kalachuvadu Publications
This translation first published in India in 2025 by Hachette India
(Registered name: Hachette Book Publishing India Pvt. Ltd)
An Hachette UK company
www.hachetteindia.com

1

Cover design and inside illustrations by Harshavardhan Behura.

Author photograph from the Sahitya Akademi website.
Translator photograph by Ramakrishnan V.

Hardback ISBN 978-93-5731-528-9
Paperback ISBN 978-93-5731-342-1
eBook ISBN 978-93-5731-772-6

Hachette Book Publishing India Pvt. Ltd
4th & 5th Floors, Corporate Centre,
Plot No. 94, Sector 44, Gurugram 122003, India

Typeset in Dante MT Std 12/17.5
by R. Ajith Kumar, New Delhi

Printed and bound in India
by Manipal Technologies Limited

FSC www.fsc.org MIX Paper | Supporting responsible forestry FSC™ C043100

Cruel is the arrow straight, the crooked lute is sweet,
Judge by their deeds the many forms of men you meet.

– *Thirukkural 279*, translated by G.U. Pope

Contents

Translator's Note

KRISHNA PARUNTHU IS A NOVEL THAT REVEALS A FRESH perspective with every reading. Having read it twice before the opportunity of translating the novel came to me, I went through it again just before I began the project. But nothing prepared me for the revelations that were in store as I unravelled one passage after another in the process of translating the text. Portions I had barely assigned any significance to during my previous readings gained prominence, highlighting not only Aa. Madhavan's attention to narrative construction but also the care needed in capturing those moments in translation. Although a realist novel, it read like detective fiction during translation, springing surprises and new discoveries every few pages. In that sense, my fourth reading of the novel – during translation – was by far the deepest.

Aa. Madhavan's prose reflects his era and his immediate surroundings. He inherited his father's business, a utensil shop, at Chaalai Bazaar in Trivandrum and wrote Tamil stories set against the backdrop of the market and its immediate neighbourhood. Since his narratives focused on Tamil people in Trivandrum, his language has a curious mix of Malayalam and Tamil. The period captured in the novel also coincides with a phase of rapid social and political change in Kerala, which Madhavan witnessed at close quarters. Therefore, the Malayalam words and the political contexts, for which I had presumptuously given my own interpretations during my previous readings, needed revisiting. I should thank Sneha, Arunima and Aarathi, my peers from the University of Madras, for their prompt inputs with Malayalam words and culture-specific ideas.

Choosing the English title for the novel was always going to be a challenge. Krishna Parunthu, or the brahminy kite, is a revered bird in south India, unbeknownst to itself. Equated to Garuda from the Ramayana, this bird of prey signifies Lord Vishnu, and people often touch their cheeks in prayer whenever they spot the bird. While a brahminy kite does make a brief appearance in the novel, it is this cultural significance of the bird that echoes in the title of the novel. Again, the seemingly simple title revealed layers of meaning when it came to translation, opening my eyes to nuances I had not considered until then. Since further discussion of the Tamil or the translated title might reveal and spoil the plot, I leave it to the readers to discover its significance. I hope the chosen title for the translation resonates with the readers by the end of the novel.

I extend my gratitude to the Tamil Nadu Textbook and Educational Services Corporation, in particular to Mini Krishnan and Dr Sankara Saravanan for giving me this opportunity to translate this novel. I am ever-grateful to my professor R. Azhagarasan, whose friendly company and guidance continue to shape me as a translator and teacher. I thank my dear friend Aadhavan Pazhani for introducing this novel to me and for all those hours of casual discussions and analyses that came in handy during translation. I am indebted to the editorial team at Hachette Book Publishing India Pvt. Ltd for their meticulous editing, and adding clarity and elegance to the translation.

PART I

1

'IS GURUSWAMY AT HOME?'

Guruswamy thought he heard a voice outside. Leaving the book he was reading on the stool, he went out to the terrace and looked at the street below.

Parvathi, generally untidy and with dishevelled hair, looked up. She was sitting downstairs on the pial smeared with cow dung and picking stones out of rice.

'Did someone ask for me, Parvathi?'

'No, Saami Aiya. No one has been here,' she replied, returning mechanically to the rice winnow again.

The poor naive creature...

Pushing aside this sympathetic thought about her, Guruswamy stood on the terrace a little longer. No one had called his name. What was happening? Lately, when he was deep in thought or lost in a book, this had been occurring quite often. Was it a subconscious yearning for someone to call out to him? What yearning could it be? Was he harbouring a craving unknown to himself? Was all his secret reading just a means to scratch at the itch of that longing? Guruswamy shook his head to scatter these thoughts. From where he was, he could see the two tall king coconut trees that stood like an arch to the farm and the Devi temple's yard thatched with palm leaves. Right behind the temple was a vast coconut grove. And on the lone giant tree beyond the grove, a brahminy kite arrived every evening, soon after sunset. There was no sign of it today. Usually, wherever he was, when it arrived to perch on the branch, he felt a sense of being watched. If he came out of the house at that time, he could usually spot the bird on that branch, turning its head this way and that, preening its feathers with its beak and screeching – like a nail being scratched on a rock. He would absentmindedly touch his cheeks in a gesture of prayer and move on to other thoughts. But the kite was not to be seen today. Was it simply his mind playing games with him? Guruswamy's thoughts swooped down to the reality around him.

In the temple yard, the children from the street were busy playing kilithattu. In the pial of the naalukkettu house on the farm, Ravi was painting a fabric poster. 'Comrades, forward…' These words stood out in bold Malayalam letters. The next lines were illegible, having just been traced in pencil and waiting to be painted. Ravi, who earned his daily bread by painting such slogans, was also the one who painted the majestic figure of the deity Akilandeshwari on the back wall of the Devi temple. On the day Ravi painted the goddess – the one who embraced the entire universe to her bosom – and gave life to what was on Guruswamy's mind, Guruswamy remembered having a surreal dream.

Although engrossed in his painting, feeling Guruswamy's presence on the terrace and hearing him ask something, Ravi rose, shook his paintbrush, wiped his hands on a rag and came down.

'Dei, dei… Stop for a moment. Look, Saami is asking me something. I can't even hear him.' He hushed the children playing boisterously in the temple yard. Then he looked up at Guruswamy and asked, 'Yes, Saami, what is it?'

'Ravi, it's nothing. Ada, you didn't have to drop what you were doing for this! I thought I heard someone calling me. I was just asking Parvathi about it. Poor thing, what does she know! She replied casually that there was no one and went back to work again… Look at her…' Guruswamy said, his smile buried beneath his dark black beard.

'Carefree thing, isn't she? Had it been anyone else, they would've seen you as a god for feeding them three times a day… But I guess creatures like her need people like you, Saami,' Ravi said, going up to the entrance of the farm.

'There's no one around, Saami. It's Sunday. Even the laundry store and scrap shop are closed today. It's only these kids who are shouting and hooting… Dei, quiet down, will you all? Saami may be reading or doing something up there. Won't you listen?' he yelled at the children and spat out betel juice.

'I'll let you know if someone comes for you, Saami,' he said and returned to the pial to resume his work. Tilting his head a little, he inspected what he had written so far. He extracted a small paper wrapper containing crumpled betel leaves, applied a little slaked lime on the leaves, gathered a pinch of areca nuts and put them in his mouth. Reviewing his work once more, he picked up the brush from the rim of the paint tin and made a corrective stroke on a letter. He stepped back and looked at it again. 'Perfect!' He then sat down to resume his work.

Guruswamy stood on the terrace for a while and watched Ravi, smiling to himself.

2

A BEAUTIFUL EVENING. THE SUN'S GOLDEN GLOW WAS streaming through the verdant canopy of the coconut grove. The coconut fronds, ebbing and rising gracefully like the keys of a harmonium under nimble fingers, filled Guruswamy's heart with delight. That the dense coconut grove hid beneath it a noisy and chaotic bazaar named Chaalaikkadai was unimaginable. Anyone enjoying this view of the coconut fronds from the terrace would be fooled into believing it was nothing more than a dense, green grove. But what a peculiar world this lush copse concealed under its shade! What scuffles, adventures, and shams… And what an eclectic variety of people!

From atop the kapok tree that stood at the end of Kamuku Vilaagam Street with criss-crossing, crucifix-shaped branches, a cuckoo sang. How did its call reach his ears despite the commotion of the children playing kilithattu in the temple yard? Was the bird perhaps weaving a song out of the evening's yellow sunlight?

Guruswamy found himself immersed in an inexplicable flood of amorous pleasure whenever the sound of music touched his heart. The rhythmic jingle of anklets, breasts heaving in the embrace of a tight corset, *jal, jal, jal*... the sky turned a dense blue and trickled... and as he melted in this exquisite sensation, music took the shape of ragas like Srungara, Mohanam and Kalyani... Ah, ah... Guruswamy's heart became light. Was it his heart that was floating in the gentle breeze of the evening?

How many trees, what a variety of creepers and the sheer range of bird species... How beautiful this place once was! Even now, after time had gradually eaten away at its glory, how beautiful his surroundings still looked! And the bird's call was only a sliver of that splendour!

To the east, the copper roof and the gold-plated domes of the Aryasalai Temple glinted in the evening sun. New cement-roofed houses in different colours stood around the temple. Amidst the coconut trees that were strewn among the houses, there also stood a peepal tree. One could also see the tin roof of Chithra Theatre from the terrace. Behind the theatre, with houses lined on either side, lay Paattu Vilaagam Street. Oblivious to the setting sun, hens continued to sift through the trash along the street. At the end of the street, you could see children playing merrily. How delightful! There was no sign of weariness; only the excited bustle of life! One's surroundings were perhaps a product of one's mind. For someone who grumbles about everything, life remains dark. If one resolves to savour everything around him, life is a merry playground.

A roar rose from among the children playing kilithattu downstairs. The team that won was celebrating raucously, lifting their captain on their shoulders.

'Saami... Saamiyappo.'

Guruswamy turned around, shaken out of his thoughts by the voice that had climbed up the stairs and sounded at his shoulder. It was Velappan.

'Come, come... Did you come home just now? Come in...'

'Yes, just now,' Velappan said, placing the plastic basket he was carrying in a corner. 'Saamiyappo, your book lies open on the table there... Who were you watching from the terrace?'

'No one in particular... I was immersed in my reading when I thought I heard someone call me... I left the book open and came here, only to find no one at the door. Then I just stood here, captivated by how gleeful the rest of the world looks.'

'You have started philosophizing again... Stop it, Saamiyappa... Why do you keep picking at your wounds!

You have nothing else to do... It's been two days since Raani left. I was hoping you would be eager to know how things are...'

Velappan trailed off as he extracted a couple of huge red bananas, then heaped a handful of sugar on a large betel leaf and placed them all in front of Guruswamy.

'What's all this, Velappa?'

'Saamiyappa! Raani gave birth to a child early this morning,' he said excitedly.

'Adade, you were right. I had forgotten all about it... Boy or girl?'

'Thanks to your blessings, it's a boy.'

'Are the mother and child fine?'

'Fine, it was a normal delivery... But going forward, I'd prefer to take her to a private hospital like we did for Chinna Ammai. I'm not going near a government hospital for any illness. I agree I was clueless during Ammai's pregnancy. I can see clearly what is what only now... Anyway, these are delicious bananas; please have them.'

'Keep the bananas aside, I'll have them later. But look at you, two years from your wedding, your wife is still in a hospital bed after her first pregnancy... and here you are, already planning the next one!'

Velappan smiled sheepishly.

'You are a proper Nair indeed! You are still the same hare-brained fellow, aren't you? Anyway... did the doctors at the government hospital not take good care?'

'You tell me, Saamiyappa... We went to the hospital at two in the afternoon as soon as she had her pains... The monkey pod tree outside the hospital was my only company since then. Hours passed, and even by midnight, I had no word from inside. It's entirely women's rule in there, I tell you... 'Men can stay outside the gate, we'll let you know when the baby is delivered,' they bark at us... When I approached a nurse who seemed like the kindest of them all, she bustled away like a cook who had left a boiling pan of oil on the stove, saying, 'Not yet, not yet...' And here I was, worried sick, unable to go anywhere, even for food or water. At last, around four in the morning, a broad-backed nurse comes out and calls, 'Who's with the woman named Raani?' I went in. 'She's had a boy. There's nothing to worry about...' she said, showing me the red-complexioned baby bundled in her arms. I hardly caught a good glimpse of him, and she had already taken the baby inside. I decided then and there that I've had enough. Saamiyappo, I'm sure you can imagine how anxious I was... All we can do is wait outside for a word from the nurses after the wife is taken in. What do we know of the goings-on inside the hospital? You finally spot a nurse and ask her what's happening, and she snarls at you like a rabid dog! Not a bit of compassion… If someone comes to me talking of the mellowness of women, I'm going to take him straight to these nurses to prove him wrong. Devils in white uniforms, they all are! That's why I say I'd rather spend some more money at a private hospital than go through this again. The nurses there will at least have the courtesy to stop and respond to your queries. I realized only now what a hard time our Ammai must have had! In those days, facilities at hospitals weren't even as good as they are today.'

'Velappa, stop talking about all that now. Why do you have to dredge up those memories now? Don't let your mind wander there. Leave that aside. I'm glad you've learnt so much from the very first pregnancy. Anyway, what does the baby look like? Has he taken after you or your wife? Did they say when you could take him home?'

'Saamiyappo, believe me or not, I saw the baby only once. He looks just like you! A thick tuft of jet-black hair and a nose exactly like yours. She has been moved from the operating theatre to the ward. Pappa Annan's wife is now taking care of her. You know how naive she is… She's had three kids but doesn't know head from heel. My wife asks why I brought her, of all people! Who else do we have, I ask. She wanted you to be the first to know. So, I arranged lunch for her, then went to the doctor's home to thank her and came to you straight from there. Look how long it has taken! I have to start immediately... Need to take some clothes and a couple of sarees for her to change into. I'm yet to give the news to the artist downstairs. I'm not sure if Venkatachalam is back home yet. I have to inform him, too. After all, aren't these the only kins we have!'

Parvathi, who had come to the terrace with a broom in hand, asked, 'Oh, is it Velappan? Aren't you supposed to be at the hospital? Has Raani given birth?'

'It's getting dark. Let her sweep the house and go home,' Guruswamy said to Velappan as both men stepped out of the house.

Then, with his gaze fixed on something in the distance, Guruswamy responded to Parvathi: 'Raani has given birth to a boy.'

'Saamiyappo, I'll take leave then. We'll talk at length later,' Velappan called as he picked up his plastic basket and descended the stairs, not waiting for a response.

As was her routine, Parvathi tidied up the room, picking up the books and newspapers that were strewn all across the room, and arranging them in their respective places. Her eyes swept past the book that lay open on Guruswamy's table and returned to it. She shut the book determinedly and left it in a corner. She then went into the kitchen, checked if everything was in order and cleaned the room. Guruswamy was standing at the terrace, looking out into the distance when she was about to depart.

'Parvathi, take the bananas and the sugar when you leave,' he said loudly, without turning to address her.

When Guruswamy entered the house after Parvathi left, the room was quite dark. He turned on the light. The tolling of the bells at the Aryasalai Temple after the customary congregation at 6.30 p.m. echoed inside the room. At that same time, someone lit a lamp and rang the bell at the Devi temple in the grove. Guruswamy returned to the terrace, looked down at the Devi temple, and held his hands together in prayer. 'Parashakthi… Mahamaaye… Devi…'

3

GURUSWAMY LIVED ALONE. HIS WIFE, FAMILY, PLEASURES, and suffering had all become things of the past by the time he turned forty-eight.

This grove in Chaalai circle was what remained after his grandfather and father had squandered everything they had possessed. It stood on a vast two-acre piece of land. Approaching from the road, the first thing one saw was the Devi temple built in the tharavadu style, enclosed on all four sides by white walls with paintings on them. There was a long pial in the thatched temple yard. The yard's floor was made of polished cement, making it convenient for the people from the surroundings to take a catnap in the afternoons. Cups containing *vibhuti* and kumkum hung from the wooden beams. The place was filled with oil lamps. Tulsi plants and flower-laden hibiscus plants lined both sides of the yard. There were five to six thatched-roof houses behind the temple. The steps to the terrace ran close to the right side wall of the temple.

The terrace was Guruswamy's abode of mental repose. Living alone in the terrace house with simple food, a head full of thoughts and enough books to feed his mind, Guruswamy was the idol of the families that lived in the grove. He lived on the income earned through the coconut trees and the rent from the grove.

It was time for the coconut harvest. Climbing to the top of the trees, Thandaan Thangappan was picking bunches of coconuts, calling, 'Mind your heads, anyone down there?' as he dropped the bunches to the ground. When he was at the top of a tree, it was hard to make out the colour of his skin from the tree's. He always wore a black kaili as a symbol of his pilgrimage to Sabarimala. He punctuated every sentence with a 'Saami Saranam', often uttering it with an apologetic tone whenever an expletive slipped past his lips. 'Saami, there are 1,500 coconuts in total. Saami Saranam. I'll come again to pick coconuts for the next harvest. Walks like a snail, that bastard! Saami Saranam!'

Guruswamy was seated in an armchair in the temple yard, watching Thangappan pick coconuts. Guruswamy had a fit body, a pleasant face, thick eyebrows, a straight nose, a dense, black, honeycomb-like beard and dark hair with no grey, which belied his years. He had stopped wearing shirts now. A saffron-coloured cotton shawl over his torso and a pure white dhoti were all he wore. He always carried a book in his hand. Even as he sat watching Thangappan picking coconuts, his forefinger rested as a bookmark inside his book.

'Saami, are you reading the book or watching the coconuts?' Ravi, the artist, walked in towards Guruswamy after spitting the betel juice in his mouth outside the temple.

'Why don't you say anything, Saami? The coconuts are getting harvested properly. Parvathi is taking care of collecting and gathering them all. There's also Vengu Bhagavathar for help. Even Pappan has kept aside his lead plating work so that he can help with the picking. Tender coconuts go for a rupee and a half these days. That's probably why everyone is so concerned about the harvest today.'

Guruswamy gave Ravi a faint smile.

'Saami, you must try chewing betel leaves. It will add a glow to your face. You don't have to chew tobacco like I do. There are good varieties of tulsi betel leaves. Add some areca nuts to them. Even the saints in the ashram chew those leaves, you know…'

'So, artist, why do you want me to do what great men do? Are you not happy that I have clear teeth and speech?' Guruswamy laughed.

'Aiyo! I didn't mean anything like that, Saami. Chewing betel leaves adds a glow to the faces of people with high intellect. Even *Ashtanga Hridayam* says so, I hear...'

'Ravi, you are an excellent artist even if you don't chew betel leaves. You are a genius. I can certify that...'

'Saami, you resort to sarcasm whenever I say something. All right, leave that aside... I need a favour. I've been meaning to ask you this for some time now.'

Guruswamy looked at him keenly. Ravi went out to the banana grove and spat the betel juice that had collected in his mouth now. This was a gesture of respect towards Guruswamy. When he worked sitting on the pial outside his house, Ravi had the habit of spitting all over the floor near him, painting the ground a dry red. Add to this paint tins of various sizes and colours with paint dripping from the brim, seven or eight brushes and rag clothes to wipe off the paint, and one could get an idea of how disorderly his workspace was in general.

'Ravi, what's with the lengthy preamble? What do you want to ask?'

'I'll come to the point. Saami, can you spare a couple of days for me? I have a strong wish to paint a portrait of you of about six feet high and four feet wide. Your beard, eyebrows, the straight nose and those eyes – they are so much like Ramakrishna Paramahamsa's. Oh, just thinking of it fills me with excitement. Do you know how regal it will look? It won't take more than three days. I know I will succeed once I pick up a pencil. This has been gnawing at my heart for some time now…'

'Looks like Artist sir is discussing something important with Saami… I, too, have something to discuss with Saami; it won't take long.' Venkatachalam, also called Vengu Bhagavathar, arrived, interrupting the conversation. He was wearing a green coloured full-sleeve kurta, with a wide streak of holy ash on his forehead. This was not the attire he usually wore when he gave musical performances at the Chaalai Bazaar. On those occasions, he wore a turban, a kurta, and a panchakacham dhoti like Bharathiyar. He also carried a drumstick to play percussion instruments during these performances. Bharathi's moustache was the only thing he lacked.

'Yes, Venkatachala Bhagavathar, what's the matter? Is Thangappan done with all the trees? Someone has to monitor him all the time and extract work. It doesn't matter whether he is on the top of a tree or on the ground; he just keeps talking. If you let him talk, no work will get done until dusk. What is it now?'

'That's what I came here for, Saami… But it seemed like Artist was deep in discussion with you—'

'Vey, Bhagavathar! I wasn't discussing anything secretive… Please get down to business,' Ravi responded sharply.

'Aiyo! Why is Ravi sir angry? I didn't mean any offense… Let's leave it aside. Now, this is what I came to discuss with Saami… All the trees along the stream bed have been picked. Only three bunches remain on the trees on the south side of the temple. Thandaan wants to know if we can pick them, too, or if any wedding party has reserved those coconut bunches…'

'If there are coconuts on those trees, ask him to pick them too. We can't wait for wedding parties and let them ripen and fall. Um, go ahead… The sun is climbing higher… Ask him to hurry up. Divide the stem, dried fronds and husk equally among yourselves. Don't come to me fighting about these things. I leave the responsibility to you, Venkatachalam. All right, go now… Hurry up. We may have a whole grove that gives a heap of coconuts, but we still end up *buying* fronds for the thatching for houses…'

4

GURUSWAMY SMILED AT RAVI AFTER VENKATACHALAM LEFT. Although veiled by his thick beard, the smile shone in his eyes.

'Why are you smiling, Saami?'

'It's nothing. Here you are, captivated by my beard and looks, itching to do a portrait of me as if there's nothing like it in the whole wide world. Meanwhile, look at all the marvelous beings god has created around us. Take this Vengu, for instance. Could anyone guess that a man with his appearance and personality would have such habits and language? Black as coal, he adamantly wears that green kurta all the time. A saffron-coloured sindoor marking on his forehead. I'm not sure if he showers even once a week. But when you hear him sing, you know how good he is. There is exceptional clarity to his words. You know, there are a few sounds in Tamil that don't come easily even to native Tamil speakers... Most people can't distinctly pronounce the special 'zha' sound. A banana is always a 'vaalaippalam' to them, and never a 'vaazhaippazham'. They're so used to the wrong sound that, when you ask them, they sheepishly admit it has become a 'palakkam' – mind you, not 'pazhakkam.' Among such people, it is rare to see someone sing as clearly as Vengu does. You need a well-trained tongue to chant the poems composed by Arunagirinathar. You must also possess a knowledge of what those songs mean. He stands in the bazaar, chants those songs to the Malayali labourers and gives elaborate commentaries for each song as if he were a saint. He switches from singing to storytelling to performing so seamlessly… A being like him stays in one of the huts in our grove, picks coconuts, does odd jobs for his daily meal and has devoted his life to Devi. When I think of it, I can't help but smile and wonder at how playful god and his designs must be!'

'Saami, you are the one who sounds like a saint now! Don't change the topic now. I truly want to paint your portrait. Just let me know the right time for it; I'll be ready accordingly.'

'All right, but not immediately. I'll tell you when I'm free. Let's begin then. But I've been hearing complaints that you are not delivering your banners on time. Only the other day, someone from the association was making such a big fuss in the grove. Don't you have to look after your livelihood?'

'Saami, how could you, of all people, ask that? Yes, I agree, I have an artistic hand. But if banners for liquor shops and political rallies are all I have to do every day, where do I go to satiate the thirst in my mind? That's why I took up the painting job at the Devi temple last year and painted those divine forms of the deity as you instructed. I swear to god, that's when I realized who you really are. We have known Bhadrakali Devi all along only as the annihilator of evils. But you were the one who explained how she is also the one who has won over the raging fire of lust. I still remember the description you gave then. I even painted it on the inner walls of the temple... Completely naked, with full breasts and open thighs – she who holds the universe in her vagina, in her majestic form with a calm countenance after having doused the fiery fire of lust... Even so, my heart races as if in a fever when I think of it even today. Say what you want, Saami, but no amount of money can match the contentment I felt when I realized I had delivered what you had in mind. Even three or four months after I painted those deities on the temple walls, my mind was revelling from the satisfaction that the project gave me. It was a pleasure beyond words. And then, the usual hoardings for the tea shop, 'Inquilab Zindabad' and 'Unite, Comrades', and all was lost again. If not for this hunger and poverty… If only I had a field of my own, I'd not touch a hoarding again. I would immerse myself in painting a thousand deities over and over to my heart's content—'

A loud cry interrupted their conversation.

'Ravi, see what's happening there. Oh, I see a crowd… I'll come, too.'

They both walked to the coconut pile, where a crowd had now gathered.

A wide ditch belonging to the Municipal Corporation ran along one edge of the grove, forming a boundary on one side of the grove. It carried sewage from the entire village. The ditch also served as a secret toilet for some people who resided in the grove. When Guruswamy and Ravi approached, they saw Pappan and Venkatachalam struggling with a hefty man, holding his arms behind him and tying his wrists together. Thandaan Thangappan was cursing and yelling at him loudly. Parvathi stood aside with dishevelled hair and a nonplussed expression.

'Great, Saami is here. Saami, do you know what this loafer did? He was hiding behind those honeysuckle bushes beyond the ditch. No self-respecting human will dare to stand in that stench. Saami Saranam. Listen to what this low birth has done… I picked a cluster of about a dozen coconuts and dropped them near the ridge of the grove. About half of them seem to have bounced and fallen into the ditch. Saami Saranam. This clever fellow has climbed into the ditch, salvaged the coconuts and smuggled them through the thatched fence. You know me; I have the eyes of a hawk even when I'm occupied with my work on the tree. I spotted him. I climbed down the tree casually to see how far he had gone. When he climbed out of the ditch with the last coconut in hand, I caught him red-handed. He tried to throw me off and escape! Dei, I, too, am a local of this Chaalai village. Look at these hands. Calloused from climbing trees since I was eight. Saami Saranam. And you thought you could escape the grip of these hands! You only have to ask, and Saami would give you a few coconuts for free. But I say it's a sin to help bastards like you. Look at the loafer – meaty enough to feed a whole pack of wolves… To bathe in sewage for a few coconuts!'

Saami stood watching the culprit keenly. He was a well-built young man, hardly twenty years of age. His shameless, bold eyes indicated that he was from within Chaalai Bazaar. He stood erect, without a hint of shame, even after being caught in the act, as if daring them to do whatever they could.

'Who are you, pa? Where are you from?' Saami asked him.

'Ask them to untie my hands,' came the impertinent reply.

'Eda, eda, mind your tongue, or else your face will lose shape!' Ravi spat at him through clenched teeth.

'Let me go, saare! I'm not Saami's bootlicker like the rest of you. I know enough. Either untie my hands, or turn me over to the police.'

'Pappa, let him go. If all the coconuts have been confiscated, we don't have to hold him here any more. Why keep him here and create a fuss…'

'Saami, your lenience is making lowlifes like this bolder by the day,' Thangappan complained.

Once his hands were untied, the coconut thief walked away irreverently in the direction of the temple, folding his dirty dhoti above his knees and tying it around his waist, muttering threats under his breath. 'Dei, Thandaan, you trash. You'll have to come by Karumadam sometime, remember. I'll take care of you then.'

'We should've smacked him in the head,' Vengu Bhagavathar said, regaining his boldness after the thief had gone out of earshot.

'Yeah, smack him and face the consequences. He will promptly bring a couple of his men to retaliate. And then it'll be a proper war. What's worse, it'll grow into a fight between landowners and labourers. You know the current situation in Chaalai Bazaar, don't you? It's not the king's rule any more... Anyway, have you gathered all the coconuts? Where's Parvathi?'

'I'm right here, Saami. I've not recovered from the fright that the thief gave me. The size of him... I'm still reeling from the shock.'

'You reel even when a hen farts, never mind that. Saami is asking you something; answer him,' Pappan teased her.

'Yes, Saami. The coconuts have been gathered. Only the counting is pending.'

Vengu was standing in a corner now, rolling up the sleeves of his green kurta, looking visibly unnerved. Although he had spoken gallantly in front of the others, he also remembered that he had to go to the bazaar the next day, drums in hand, for his livelihood. What would he do if the coconut thief accosted him the next day at the bazaar with a couple of cronies, beat him up and took away his drums?

In some time, the regular buyers gathered at the grove. Some coconuts were kept aside first as payment for the labourers. Apart from this, every house in the grove received four coconuts each. Once he had separated these coconuts, Thangappan took charge of making the bargain with the buyers. During these sales, Guruswamy would sit calmly with a serene smile on his face.

'Saami must know the state of affairs now. It is true that the price of coconuts went up last month. But the demand has gone down this month. A shipment of copra has arrived from Ceylon recently. Oil mills are already turning us away. If we persist beyond that, they deliberately ask at a low price.' Buyers invariably attempted to bargain through such stories.

A smile was the only response from Guruswamy.

'Saami smiles happily. Of course, you know everything. All, right, I'll take all the coconuts for 110 rupees. Considering the peeling, husking and extracting labour involved, I can see some profit only at that price.'

'Thangappa?' Guruswamy called.

This was his sign to Thangappan to check the accounts and make the sale. Once the sale was done, Thangappan would leave home, taking the coconuts that had been allotted as his payment.

Such was the routine at the grove. Nothing different transpired that day. When the sale was over and Guruswamy was climbing up the stairs of his house, Parvathi was dragging the coconut fronds allotted to each house all by herself. Vengu and Pappan cleverly got out of any more work once the sale was over. To them, she was, after all, the one who was fed by Guruswamy to take care of menial tasks.

'Paaru, can you drag these fronds to our houses as well? It's been hours since my last beedi. I'll go buy a pack and be back soon,' they made excuses and hurried away.

Parvathi toiled in the sun, walking back and forth between the grove and the houses. Yes, she was a poor soul indeed.

5

PARVATHI WAS NOT THE ONLY PITIABLE CREATURE AROUND there. So was Vengu, who sang in the streets of Chaalai Bazaar for a living, and Pappan, who repaired and tinned vessels for daily bread. What about painter Ravi, who straddled the spheres of aspiration and occupation? Not to mention Velappan, who worked at the Dairy Cooperative Society. To be fair, if not for Guruswamy's plantation, their plight would have been unimaginable. Perhaps they would have become residents of the Karimadam Colony or Kalippaankulam Colony like most scoundrels of Chaalai Bazaar. In his own way, even Guruswamy was pitiful. His family was prosperous in the days of his forefathers. The plantation, in those times, was not the paltry two-acre piece of land that it was now. It was spread out on vast acres. By the time the coconut harvesting that began from one end of the plantation reached the other end, the next reaping season would have arrived, where the harvest began again. Lots of areca nuts, chillies, pepper, mangoes and jackfruits were also grown on these lands. It used to be a land that kept giving.

Anantharangam Pillai, Guruswamy's father, was bestowed the title of the 'Chief Pillai' by the king who then ruled the province. He preserved the sword presented to him by the king as an invaluable treasure until his death. But before Guruswamy reached his youth, Anantharangam Pillai had squandered three-fourths of the property left by his father, who himself had thrown away his own share of the riches. Some of it went for their concubines, some in maintaining the grandeur that was befitting the title of 'Chief Pillai' and most of it in profligacy. Guruswamy acquired a distaste for the royal pomp and the reckless extravagance of his family at a very young age and instead chose to participate in the Independence movement, crying 'Bharat Mata ki Jai' and expounding nationalism.

Today's plantation life was largely an outcome of the quiet family life he made for himself with his wife after his father's death. With obedient people around, what started off like a serene stream of life turned into a lonely boat ride after the sudden demise of his wife. What remained in his mind now was the vacuum left behind by the bright light that was once his indispensable support.

Like an archer taking aim at something in the water, his life was now confused, without ambition. Guruswamy had got used to this life now. Why? He knew why. But of what use was the knowledge when it was too late anyway? In fact, it was quite surprising that Guruswamy had a contempt for the petty desires of the flesh at a very young age – when he had the vigour of youth and his family had wealth. However, he had also experienced the occasional pangs of love during his schooldays. A particularly distasteful incident that occurred during one of those high days had sucked out the pleasures of love in him. The image continued to haunt him even when his father insisted he get married. His revulsion had stayed hidden inside him even after he married Subbulakshmi – secretly, like a kite that hides in the foliage and sheds its feathers.

Although his mother had passed away when he was just a child, there were several mother figures in the house. One among them was Ammu, a middle-aged woman who acted as Guruswamy's caretaker. 'Ammu amme… Ammu amme…' Guruswamy was quite fond of his caretaker. Ammu was an amicable woman with a pleasant face, slightly cat-like eyes and a sweet voice. She had to sing 'Aambaadi thannil ore unniyundangane', a Krishnagatha song, to make him sleep every day.

'Ammu will sing you a song now. My dear child must eat healthily.' She would coax him with a bowl of rice mixed with lentils.

'Gurumon! What did you learn at school today?' she enquired lovingly every evening when he came back from school, gathering him in a tight embrace. When he asked, 'Ammu amme! Tell me a story,' she immediately told him stories of Rani of Jhansi as if she had been waiting for him to ask. After showering every morning, she let her long, dense hair fall loose on her back, went to the temple, adorned her forehead with a streak of sandal paste and woke him up with an embrace when she got home. With the scent of the hot oil and the fragrant flowers on her hair, she reminded him of the wish-granting fairies from stories. He found that same fairy on his father's bed one day, naked and exposed, playing with the grey hair on his father's bare chest, playfully biting his thick, betel-reddened lips… and more disgusting things… Aiyo… Chi… Ammu ammov! *How filthy! I don't need you any more. I'll let no one touch me hereafter. I don't need anyone. I don't want anything.*

Was it that revulsion that transformed him into this ascetic-like figure, living in the plantation, surrounded by his acolytes? Although people around him called him 'Saami', he knew there was a kite soaring in the depths of his heart. The kite perched on the branches of trees that were within his sight during his meditations on the terrace in the evenings.

'...it all ends up at the plantation. Poor man, Guruswamy,' was often quoted in that region. The plantation was on the street that went north from the road that ran from Chaalai Bazaar to Aryasalai. The street branched into long, dark alleys full of scrap recycling businesses and tinker shops – handling a variety of articles like tin vessels, pulleys, old newspapers and jute bags. Then there was the Angalamman Temple street. Walking eastwards down this road, one could find another street branching north. This one led to Kamuku Vilaagam Street, Paattu Vilaagam Street and Thampanoor Railway Station. Midway on this street, just before where Kamuku Vilaagam Street began, the plantation lay on the left. The surrounding was ruined by gutters full of sewage, teeming with fish and human waste, and garbage dumps. Yet, many passers-by on that road stopped at the entrance of the plantation, removed their footwear and worshipped Devi before they went on their way. From there, the deity's form could be seen dimly under the thatched roof of the temple. Even the hibiscus and tulsi plants in the yard and the large painting of the deity on the temple wall were visible from there.

Everyone from that region feared Devi. In Guruswamy's words, 'Fear is devotion.' Wasn't it?

There were six houses in the grove now. In fact, these 'houses' were merely thatched-roof huts. After his wife died, leaving him with no children, Guruswamy trimmed and altered the palatial house of his forefathers into a modest abode. In this double-storey house with the stairs to the first floor set inside, he partitioned the ground floor space overlooking the road into three portions and let them out for rent. Three shops stood there now: a laundry shop, a ration shop and a small shop that sold betel leaves and areca nuts. Even for these shops, Guruswamy collected a considerably lower rent compared to the usual rates at Chaalai Bazaar. The house on the first floor had a living room with smooth, red cement flooring. There was a small kitchen and a bathroom inside. To the left of the living room, there was another room that was Guruswamy's pooja and store room. Every morning, after his shower, he went into the room with just a wet towel around his waist. After about fifteen minutes of absolute silence, the fragrance of sandal incense filled the house, following which Guruswamy stepped out of the room. He picked his dhoti from the clothesline, wore it and went into the kitchen next. He boiled the milk that Parvathi would have kept ready. He also boiled a banana or settled for bread and jam for breakfast. Then he went to the living room and read the day's newspapers, combing his beard constantly with one hand. The wall opposite him in the living room was adorned with portraits of Gandhi, Buddha, Ramakrishna Paramahamsa and E.V.R. Periyar. On the far end of the wall, there was a huge eight-by-six portrait of a nude woman. It was painted by Kunjikkuttan Thambiraan, an artist of an old king's court. It was now so faded that a new visitor may not be able to immediately make out the subject of the painting. But for someone who cared enough to stand there and pay close attention, everything would be clear. Guruswamy also had a large collection of books that one could not finish reading in a lifetime. He read all the time. For lunch, he had boiled rice. He had a few powders of curry handy in the kitchen. Parvathi sometimes brought chopped vegetables or greens to be cooked and had with the rice. Guruswamy was particularly fond of greens. So, a variety of greens could always be found growing in the yard amidst the hibiscus plants all year round.

Parvathi knew how much Guruswamy loved kuzhambu made with greens and lentils. However, Guruswamy mostly cooked for himself. Parvathi took whatever was left after he had had his meal. She also washed the dishes, cleaned the kitchen top and kept the house clean. That was all she knew. With dishevelled hair, dark skin and wearing a saree whose colour was not distinguishable anymore, Parvathi went around naively with a funny gait and even a funnier way of talking.

Parvathi had worked as a maid here even when Guruswamy's wife was alive. Although Parvathi was needed for everything, from daily shopping and laundry to accompanying her to the occasional temple visit, Guruswamy's wife never let her inside the house. After Subbulakshmi passed away, when people asked him to replace the hideous and naive maid with someone presentable, Guruswamy curtly said, 'She's good enough.'

'Saami is not keen on employing any other woman. What if they get pregnant through someone, and shift the blame on Saami with the intent of extracting money from him? Why take such risks? Saami is not so old that he can't remarry. Who'll dare to deny giving their girl if you wish to remarry?' people often commented.

Guruswamy's response was always the same: 'I've experienced married life enough. How many women my father married, and how many more mistresses he had! What was the use of it all? Here I am, his only heir. So, Parvathi's services are enough for this household. Whether it is me or Parvathi or the priestess of the Iyengar Mutt, we are all the same to our deity, Devi.

Think about it yourself... When there are so many of us residing in this grove, who does Devi choose particularly to descend upon? It is on Parvathi, isn't it? Then why should we feel an aversion towards someone whom even our deity deigns to be worthy?'

Guruswamy felt the same way about everyone in the neighbourhood. Be it Parvathi, the naive maid, or Velappan, the labourer of the Dairy Cooperative Society, or Ravi, the artist, or Vengu, the street singer, or Pappan, the tinsmith, all of them were equal recipients of Guruswamy's love, compassion and trust.

'We know you are compassionate. But can't you at least collect a nominal rent from the residents in the grove? You also give away coconuts and fronds to them. How foolish! You won't find such things happening anywhere else on earth. By today's rates, each cent of land easily goes for six or seven thousand rupees. Remember that land next to the stream? The one your father sold for two or three thousand rupees a long time ago? Sait has built two line houses on that land now and rented them out for a hundred and fifty or two hundred,' a well-wisher once broached the topic.

'As if I've lost a fortune by not collecting rent for these thatched huts! They are poor folks; let them be. Sait has a large family to take care of, and correspondingly great expenses. What am I going to spend on? I don't have children either. I have not earned even a paisa of this wealth I have. It's all inherited from my ancestors. What was once acres of land has now dwindled to this after my grandfather and father splurged it on their wives, mistresses and royal lifestyles. Now, I am the lone inheritor of what is left. I do have some relatives somewhere. But to them, I am a madman. I have a strange personality. No one knows what I think. I'm also almost fifty now. Yes, I got a primary education. But my father was not a great person. Something disturbed me at a very young age, and I dropped out of school. Whatever 'reading' I have came later – after my involvement with the nationalist movement. When my father kept badgering me about getting married, the movement helped me evade it for a while. Eventually, when I married Subbulakshmi, I was thirty. Poor girl, she put up with me so patiently for almost seven years! She lost three children in the maternity ward and passed away herself with the third one. People said all kinds of things… Some said Devi was angry at us for occupying her temple's yard. Some said my grandfather and father had desecrated the temple with their corrupt ways. Devi Amma is not to be blamed. We worship her, and the only way we can show her our devotion is by not making her a witness to our depravity. I've become a 'saint' now because I speak this way! Yes, I have a thirst to read a lot. I keep reading. I feel too lazy to even shave. Now, the beard has also become a symbol of my piety.'

6

THE GROVE WAS PARTICULARLY LIVELY THAT MORNING. Parvathi had risen early as usual, bathed in the Chenthitta Devi Temple pond, washed her clothes, adorned her forehead with kumkum and entered her hut to hang the wet clothes on the clothesline. Venku, who had bathed even before Parvathi, was in a bright white dhoti, looking into a palm-sized mirror and applying a streak of sandal on his forehead.

'Parvathi, looks like you're a little late today? I woke up at four and went for a bath in the Killiyaaru River. Where is Velappan? Has he already gone to work? He wouldn't have gone today, would he? Is he still asleep?'

'Who knows!' Parvathi gestured with open palms and walked north towards Velappan's house. The hibiscus plant in the yard was so full of flowers that the leaves were hardly visible. Since it was still early in the morning, the flowers had not bloomed fully yet. Parvathi stood staring at the flowers for some time.

Raani was sitting with her baby lying on her outstretched legs, bathing it with lukewarm water. The baby cried out as soon as water touched its body. 'Lo, lo... That's all, that's all... I'm not hurting you, see... Let's clean you up...' Raani crooned to placate the baby. When she saw that Parvathi was at the door, she said, 'Oh, there you are! It's six already. He woke up early and went to take a bath. He's still not home. Ever since the baby came, nothing gets done at home. It's an auspicious day, and I haven't even swept the house front or drawn a kolam yet. If he comes home now, he'll fly into a rage. I had planned to give the baby a nice warm bath on the day of his paandu sutthu, you know, the purification ceremony. In the short gap that I left him in the cradle and went to fetch water from the tank, he had soiled himself and rolled in it. Parvathi, can you take care of cleaning up the temple yard? It's only the twenty-eighth day today. I'm not allowed to go outside the house until after the paandu sutthu. I've been able to manage so far only because of you and Pappan Anna's wife. Can't thank her enough... She's been making porridge and food for us. I was the one who told my husband I'll take care of everything and that I didn't need any help. That's why I'm worried he'll be furious when he returns to find things in this state…'

'I took care of tidying the temple yard and drawing the kolam at three in the morning. Why do you worry about all that, Raani? Do I need to be told these things? Who will do it for Devi if not me? I'll leave, then. I have to sweep Saami's room before he wakes up. I don't know if the milkman has come yet. Have to keep the vessel ready to collect milk.' Parvathi walked briskly towards Guruswamy's house. Pappan was squatting outside his house, fresh out of bed and yawning but busy with some brass vessels, bellows and charcoal spread out in front of him. His wife was still asleep on the pial, with her saree draped around her like a blanket. Their ten- and eight-year-old children were asleep on the bare floor. A dark, oil-stained pillow lay a few feet away.

The sound of a hammer could be heard from the blacksmith's workshop around the corner. Several crows were cawing raucously from atop the electric line that ran along the road. A raven hung like a black rag from the lamp post, probably electrocuted when it perched on the pole.

As Parvathi climbed the stairs in Guruswamy's house, Ravi came from the south after his morning routines, clad in a baniyan and lungi, with an empty bucket in hand.

He said, 'Pappan, you seem to have set up your shop so early in the morning! Quite a labourer indeed... Leave aside the paandu sutthu arranged for Velappan's child. Have you also forgotten today is the day of the kaappu festival at our Devi temple? Come now, pack everything up.'

'Artist sir! Why are you making such a ruckus so early in the morning? You don't have a family or children to take care of like I do. You've left your wife at her parents' place and visit her once in a while. Can I live like you? I have to do my work every day to keep the family afloat. Will I ever forget our Devi's festival? Or will I forget Velappan's precious child, who was born two years after their marriage? These are my responsibilities, too! Velappan is a trusted aide of Saami... Saami is so close to us all... Anyway, I'll wrap up soon,' Pappan responded, even as he was busy cutting out the corroded portion of a brass pan.

'If you had been this sincere a couple of days ago, maybe you would've had time today to prepare for the festival,' Ravi said, putting down the bucket and extracting betel leaves from the folds of his lungi.

'Oh, Artist sir! I know how sincere you are with your

work. I was right here when the proprietor of the textile shop made several trips here, enquiring about his shop hoarding. I was here when he eventually yelled at you and when you placated him. 'You'll have it by noon tomorrow,' you said to him. Tell me, in the name of Devi, have you written at least a letter for that hoarding? That's the case with us labourers. We dread the fire only after we're burnt, don't we?'

'All right, all right… Finish up and come soon. Two plantain trees were brought yesterday evening. With a couple more hands for help, we can tie them up as an arch at the Devi temple's entrance. Look there! Velappan is here at last – bathed and prim as a priest!'

The golden sun was rising between the coconut trees beyond the pillar of the Aryasalai Temple.

'Artist sir has not freshened up yet? The sun is already rising,' Velappan asked as he entered his house with washed wet clothes on his shoulder.

Guruswamy had just woken up and come out to the terrace. He stood there, watching the sun rise. The sun's golden rays danced magically in his eyes. From his eyes, they entered his thoughts, from his thoughts to his mind, and from there, to every nerve inside him. 'Ammu amme! Please sing 'Aambaadi thannil ore unniyundangane.' Of course, you won't sing to me… You prefer to sleep with my old father... Why don't you sing, Ammu amme? Please sing...' Tears rolled down from her cat-like eyes. 'Ammu amme, don't cry!' But her nakedness... Her ample breasts like that of the painting on the Devi temple's wall – the Devi who held the entire universe in her vagina, the one who doused the fire of lust, the one who ruled the world... 'Ammu amme!' Ammu amme descended from the golden rays of the sun... She came down softly, carefully, like a cradle's gentle movement... She came closer... Who was it? Was it his wife, Subbulakshmi? No... Raani stood there with her baby in her arms.

'Saamiyappo, you're worshipping the sun longer than usual today! It's past seven already.'

When he looked down from the terrace, Raani stood there smiling at him, cradling the freshly bathed baby in her hands. At first, everything looked like a shadow... Like babies of the sun... When he blinked a few times and rubbed his eyes, he could clearly see Raani, the baby and the thatched roof. She was in the backyard of her house, where little yellow flowers had withered off the coconut trees. Velappan came out with a soft towel and collected the baby in his arms. He looked up at the terrace and asked, 'Saamiyappo, haven't you finished your morning routines yet? It's your grandson's paandu sutthu day today. Also, the kaappu festival for Devi. Have you forgotten?'

'Oh, you and your mouth! Grandson, it seems. Don't make Saamiyappo an old man already. My brother, Das, and Saamiyappa are of the same age. He's my baby's uncle,' Raani retorted, gathering the baby from Velappan.

'Oh, of course, you'll never forego your family. I don't mind how my son addresses our Saamiyappa.'

'You two don't have to bicker about this on an auspicious day. Let him grow up and call me anything. Who knows, he may choose to call me Saamiyappo like everyone does. I'd like that, too. Get on with your work. I'll finish my shower and come. If Parvathi comes, ask her to buy nendran bananas from the shop at the end of the street. I have already asked them to keep it ready.'

How was I able to switch from those intense thoughts to such mundane affairs so quickly? he wondered as he descended the stairs and walked towards the garden. Parvathi was sitting on the pial of the temple, busy making a garland out of hibiscus flowers and tulsi leaves, unaware of Guruswamy crossing her and heading towards the back of the temple.

'Saami is passing by, and there she sits, completely blind to what's going on around her!' Pappan pointed out to his wife.

'Uh hum,' she said and spat out the coal with which

she was brushing her teeth.

'Ass! Look who I'm talking to about her! You are a close second to her, after all.'

Guruswamy stopped behind the temple and stood watching the Shri Chakra on the back wall. The morning sun was rising, warming up the surroundings.

7

ALL THE LAMPS IN THE DEVI TEMPLE WERE FILLED WITH OIL, and the white wicks were alight with flame. Two gas lamps were lit up, one at the entrance to the grove and the other in the temple yard.

'We may have bright electric lamps and fluorescent tubes, but they cannot always be relied on. For auspicious days like these, there is nothing more fitting than a couple of bright, hissing gas lamps!' Velappan remarked enthusiastically.

It was still twilight. The deepa aaradhanai was scheduled for after eight in the evening. Usually, all lights in the temple were lit, and a special deepa aaradhanai was conducted every Tuesday and Friday. Patrons sometimes presented puttu or aravanaipayasam to the deity and then distributed them to the devotees. Children from Kamuku Vilaagam, Paattu Vilaagam and Karikkadai Corner gathered regularly at the temple yard to receive these offerings. Some older children occasionally sang the 'Simha Vaahini' song. Vengu Bhagavathar also sang songs in praise of Devi in a loud voice, which children repeated after him. With all this happening before the deepa aaradhanai, one hardly felt the time passing.

The Devi temple premises had a festive glow that day. Half a dozen bunches of bananas were placed on the clean pial of the temple. The temple pillars were decorated with bunches of red coconuts from the grove. Vengu generally gained a new vigour when it came to festivals at the Devi temple. After all, his livelihood was singing songs about Devi, Lord Muruga and various saints. Bright white streaks of holy ash shone on his forehead, chest, arms and elbows as he ran around busily. Artist Ravi could be found helping Potri, the man from Sabapathi Street, who usually decorated the deity. He took care of preparing the sandal paste, powdering charcoal for decoration and passing on the sandal and kumkum to Potri whenever needed. Potri fixed a pair of silver eyes on Devi's face and then clipped a plastic pearl nose ring to the tip of her nose. The gilded crown on her head glittered in the bright light. Since the walls around the statue were adorned with mirrors, the light reflecting off the wall surface accentuated the smooth features of

Devi's face. On the south corner, with a long, wooden-handled ladle in hand, Pappan was mixing the jaggery pongal that was cooking in a large pan set on an equally large brick stove. Wearing a red towel around his waist and a white towel around his head, he had transformed into a neat and tidy chef. Amidst all this commotion, Parvathi sat quietly on the temple pial under the light of an oil lamp, stringing a garland. What singular focus she had! Her deep devotion had brought a unique grace to her otherwise naive countenance. Was this the same Parvathi who climbed Guruswamy's staircase every day, wearing a dirty saree hitched above her knee, armed with a broom and an old bucket? Was she the Parvathi who raced with Pappan's little children to collect the coconut fronds that fell from the trees? Was she that same woman who waited outside Raani's house with an aluminium bowl in hand, calling, 'Raaniyammov, I'm starving… Bring some salted porridge diluted in water, please?' Was this the creature who bathed in the Chenthitta Temple pond very early every morning, cold or rain, and circumambulated the temple, trembling from head to toe? Was this the same Parvathi who went into a trance during the deepa aaradhanai time, shaking and shouting violently before falling unconscious like a felled plantain tree? Was she finding salvation by stringing garlands for Devi? There she sat, focused, her fingers carefully and nimbly moving around the flowers as if they were sparrows picking grains off the sand.

At times like these, it was remarkable how people worked in unity. Children and women had come not only from Guruswamy's plantation, Kamuku Vilaagam and Paattu Vilaagam Street but also from Chaalai, Ilavaaniya Street, and Karuppatti Market Street. There were even a few Kammala and Malayali women. Velappan stood at the front of the crowd gathered at the temple. He had brought a wicker basket full of popcorn and transferred it to a sack in one corner of the temple. 'Are the percussionist and the musicians not here yet? It's past seven, ne!' he asked Venku. Without waiting for an answer, he hurried towards the street.

'He takes great care and responsibility when it comes to his family affairs, doesn't he?' Ravi remarked to the priest.

'Of course, he does! They're blessed with a child after a long wait. Besides, he is close to Guruswamy and resides close to the Devi temple. He once used to go from house to house to milk the cows in each household. Then he secured this properly paying job at the Dairy Society. In fact, it was after he got that job that he was blessed with a child. So, I guess he's thankful for all the good things that have come his way now. There's no surprise that he's so involved, is there?'

'Oh, what do you know about him! He chases after money. I've seen him since his childhood days. He used to milk money out of Guruswamy for everything. A dangerous fellow, he is. After all, he's a Malayali, isn't he? Malayalis generally wear a bright smile, as bright as their clothes. But deep inside, they are as stubborn as iron. He could not have dreamt of marrying Raani had it not been for Saami. Even if he had, he could not have found this secure life he has in the grove.'

'Oi, Artist, stop it now! We're in the middle of a festive occasion. Let's not speak ill words,' Potri interrupted, mounting a parrot made of dye-soaked cotton on Devi's hand. He then stepped back to see if everything was fine. 'Now she looks exactly like Madurai Meenakshi!' he gushed proudly.

'Saami, I just said the truth. They're not ill words if they're true. Anyway, let it be... Isn't Guruswamy at home? I didn't see him around, even during the day. But the lights are on at his house. Maybe he's lost in his reading? I'm telling you, I've seen a lot of men, I've heard about some pretty weird cases. But I've never come across anyone like him! Always so lost in his books. He may not even notice if his roof is on fire! I see little children these days wearing eyeglasses because they read all the time. But look at him. He must be close to fifty – the age around which people so commonly get cataracts. And yet, he reads day and night, as healthy as ever… I've been waiting for a good opportunity. I would like to do a full-size oil painting of him seated in a throne-like chair. Mark my words. With the blessings of Devi, I'll paint that masterpiece one day. He has even given his consent, you know.'

'Fine, fine… Enough talking. If Parvathi is done with the garlands, bring the geranium one and one strung with assorted flowers. If only we had procured some screw pine, too! I checked everywhere in Chaalai Bazaar. I know this is not the season. Still, you can't blame a man for hoping… Look, Velappan is back. Oi, come here! Where are the musicians? Do you know what the time is?'

'Potri Saami, that's what I've been worried about, too. I went to the Aryasalai Temple to enquire. The musicians there say they will be able to come here only after their temple is closed for the day. Haa… There comes our musician! Come soon… Where have you people been? Do you know how late it is?'

'What's the time now? You asked us to come after seven. It's only seven-thirty now, isn't it?'

'Never mind... Get started with the melam. Let everyone gather.'

The moment the musicians began their performance, the temple premises acquired a festive glow. People who were scattered on the street and in front of the betel leaf shop came together at the entrance of the temple. The women were gathered in the yard on the north side, where hibiscus and henna plants grew. A few children were playing in the sand, under the bright glow of the gas light. Pappan's wife was chatting with a few women from Angalamman Street, which was where she had grown up. She looked bright in a clean cotton saree and a green jumper. It was bright as day in the yard lit by the gas lamp and electric lights. Guruswamy stood on his terrace majestically, wearing a thin towel on his shoulders, a plain white dhoti and kumkum on his forehead. An amused smile played on his lips behind the thick, black beard. He noticed that there were more women than men in the crowd. *Only women go to the cinema and temples these days,* he thought. He scanned the crowd for Raani's family members. No point looking for them there. Since Das and his family blamed Guruswamy for everything that had happened between Velappan and Raani, there was no way they would set foot in his plantation again. Poor Raani! She was a fine girl – the sister of his old friend,

Das. She had fought against her entire family in order to marry Velappan, and now she was a mother to a child. The things that love made people do!

Raani's family possessed riches that could last for three or four generations. If she had married someone chosen by her family, she could have lived the life of a queen now. But she threw it all away and eloped with Velappan, who belonged to a different caste, in addition to being just a servant at her house. They say passion is short-lived, but it was not true in Raani's case. She showed no regret at having sacrificed a luxurious life. How happy she was! What a stark difference there was between the stories of exaggerated divine love or lustful passion that he read in books and the story of love he witnessed in front of his very eyes! Guruswamy was not aware of the extent of luxury that Raani had left behind, but he was witness to the happy and contented life she led under the thatched roof of the hut. Guruswamy thought that perhaps down the line, when she had three or four more children and struggled to make ends meet, she might wonder what her life could have been. Was Raani also like countless devotees who prayed when they saw a brahminy kite? 'Aha, there flies a brahminy kite! How high it soars… That white neck behind which Lord Mahavishnu will be seated… Parandhaama, bless us!' People often touched their cheeks reverently when they sighted the kite. Did Raani see Velappan as a brahminy kite who could bring fulfillment to her life? As Guruswamy stood thinking about Raani, was something blooming in his heart?

8

AMIDST THE BOOM OF THE MELAM, THE AIR WAS FILLED with the fragrance of incense, flowers and sandal. Parvathi stood near the pial, with closed eyes and folded hands, lost in prayer. How was this shabby creature able to dive into such deep levels of meditation at times like this? How devoted she was, and what reverence there was behind those closed eyes! Whether there was a God or not, such intense meditation had its own powers. It gave you singular focus, blurring everything else around you. It helped you fix your mind on one thing without distractions. The story of Sanandanan – the son of this very land – also speaks of the power of this heightened state of meditation, doesn't it? Sanandanan was a scholar and hermit. He sat in deep prayer in the forest, wishing to see the Narasimha incarnation of Lord Vishnu. It was such an intense prayer that the heat he emanated could have dried up the seas. But what happened eventually? The lord never appeared in front of him. A nomadic hunter named Saatthan felt pity for the emaciated hermit and pleaded to him, 'What is it that you are praying for? Cruel time has started building a termite hill around you! What is it that you want, Swami? If it is within my reach, I can bring it to you.'

Sanandanan found the poor hunter's compassion funny. 'Oh, dear hunter, you are right on at least one count. It is indeed an animal that I'm praying for. It's Narasimha – a being with a human body and the head of a lion. Can you bring him to me?'

'What did you call it, Swami?'

'Narasimha,' the hermit responded curtly and resumed his deep prayer.

Saatthan immediately went looking for the strange animal. He scoured every inch of the forest, hills and caves. Unable to find an animal that matched the hermit's description, Saatthan was vexed. 'I wish to capture the beast before the hermit loses his life. Oh, Narasimha! Where are you? My dear beast, where can I find you?' he cried out madly. He roamed around the forest without food or sleep, calling out to Narasimha all the while. Lord Vishnu, who was deep in slumber, was awakened by the fervency with which Saatthan pursued Narasimha. He appeared in front of Saatthan in a miniature form of Narasimha. Elated beyond words, Saatthan leashed the little animal with a rope made out of grass and headed straight to Sanandanan. The lord went along with him like a domesticated cat. 'Swami, look here! I've brought the Narasimha you were looking for. Open your eyes,' he called.

When Sanandanan opened his eyes, there stood Lord Narasimha, with a beatific smile, and calling out to him: 'Sanandana!'

'Lord, I have been praying to you for decades together now. How did you, who have not appeared before my eyes this long, agree to be leashed by a mere hunter?'

'Sanandana! You attempted to summon me with your ego. Your intense prayers fell like snow rather than flow like a deluge that could wash me away towards you. This Saatthan, on the other hand, came looking for me sincerely, with the only objective of helping you. I had no alternative but to appear in front of him.'

'Swami! My ego has been slayed,' Sanandanan cried, falling at his feet.

Parvathi was a pure soul, like Saatthan, the hunter. Even the percussionist, having sensed that she was guileless, was deliberately playing his melam close to her ears.

Raani stood in the temple yard, carrying the baby in a cushion of fresh clothes. Had she gained a gleam after her pregnancy? A couple of teenagers in the crowd pointed at Raani in the middle of their conversation and giggled among themselves. When they realized that Guruswamy was watching from the terrace, the boys quietly shifted into the crowd and disappeared. The baby in Raani's arms was sleeping with its rose-red fists clenched. There was a woollen cap with a pom-pom on its little head. How had Velappan thought of buying these things? Perhaps he had naturally gained a sense of responsibility when he became a family man. Guruswamy had no children. That was perhaps why he lived a life without care – not worried about money or earnings, content with reading his books, watching the sun rise and set, listening to the music in the cacophony of birds, worshipping the kite that perched on the tree branch to rest after a long day's flight. In fact, Subbulakshmi bore children. After giving birth to two children who died soon after they were born, she, too, passed away with the third. Was that the reason behind his deep-seated aversion to everything?

The tinkling of the temple bells denoting the beginning of the pooja could be heard despite the sound of the drums. The musician with the naayanam switched to a higher note, lifted the instrument skywards and played it with renewed energy. And then came Vengu's voice, loud and clear, singing a mellifluous song about Devi.

The scene was bound to give anyone goosebumps. How carefully they had picked words and strung them together into a melody! How beautifully Vengu – who usually went around like a grimy beggar – sang it with such devotion and clarity. After all, it was this bold, unfettered voice that earned him his daily bread. Although he was a Malayali, the beauty and clarity of his Tamil pronunciation invariably drew people in the market towards him. He could often be found in the crowded section of the market, clad in his usual kurta, dhoti, a turban like Bharathi's and a black bead necklace around his neck, playing his drums, singing a Thiruppugazh verse, and what more, following it up with a commentary as well. Crowds thronged wherever he was, donating various denominations ranging from ten paise to a rupee. By the time he came a full circle around the market, he would have earned enough for a week's survival. Although the songs he sang were composed by divine poets, Vengu possessed the rare talent of presentation that captivated his audience.

The crowd at the temple was now spellbound by Vengu's song. Raani placed the baby on the fresh palm-leaf mat that was laid on the temple yard. The priest emerged from within the sanctum sanctorum with a small vessel of water on which a couple of tulsi leaves floated. He scooped a spoonful of the water, transferred it to his palm and sprinkled it on the baby in a gesture of blessing. Startled by the sudden shower, the baby began to wail loudly. The women gathered around immediately began ululating. 'Where's the baby's father?' the priest called.

Velappan ran to Guruswamy and invited him forward. 'Saami, please come. We're going to tie the sacred thread for the baby. I want you to stand at the front and bless him.'

When Velappan tied the silver string around the crying baby's waist, Guruswamy brought his hands together on his chest, closed his eyes and prayed.

Pappan encouraged the women around to ululate once again. With the sounds of the ululations, the melam and the naayanam, the temple turned festive.

Potri, the priest, handed the baby back to Raani and said, 'Take a pinch of Devi's kumkum and wear it on your forehead. The baby has been wailing for some time now. Take it aside and feed it some milk or water. It's time for the deepa aaradhanai.'

Parvathi, who had been standing as quiet as a shadow with shut eyes and folded hands, squealed suddenly. Her body began shaking, although she remained rooted where she was. 'Um... Um...' she grunted from time to time.

'Devi has descended upon Parvathi... Move aside, everyone!' Ravi, Vengu and Pappan busied themselves with keeping the converging crowd at bay. The melam and the naayanam continued to resound.

'Let her be! Where is the lamp plate? Bring some more holy ash... It's time for the deepa aaradhanai!' the priest called out, lighting the small mound of camphor on the lamp plate. He waved the plate in circles – from the foot of the Devi statue to its face. What a divine face it was! What elegance even the ghastly face of the statue possessed! Guruswamy stood transfixed, his heart swelling in devotion, his eyes consuming the glow emanating from the deity.

'Oh, mother of the universe! Oh, Devi, the queen of all worlds!' he prayed.

After swaying in a trance for some time, Parvathi screeched and fell unconscious to the floor like a felled tree. Pappan's wife and a couple of women from the bazaar lifted her and laid her to rest on the pial of a house nearby. One of the women sprinkled cold water on Parvathi's face and also fed her some water. Another woman fanned her face with a palm-leaf fan.

When they stopped playing the melam and naayanam, a still silence settled everywhere. In the bright light thrown by the lamps, a throng of lively faces...

The noise of the crowd picked up again when it was time to distribute the prasadham, the sacred food that was laid at the deity's feet earlier. With a bronze pot in one hand and a ladle in another, Velappan was serving pongal to the women. After the birth of his child, he had shaved off his beard, trimmed his hair, moustache and sideburns and become more presentable. It showed on his face when he served the prasadham among the women. After a brief chat with a young girl, he served a generous amount of paayasam, the sweet porridge, on the leaf she carried in her palms.

'Velappa, looks like you're offering the prasadham based on the receiver's face?' Ravi remarked with a mischievous grin.

'What am I going to accomplish now, looking at girls? She's like a younger sister to me. Then should I not offer her some extra prasadham? Anyway, why does it bother the artist now?'

'Oh, I'm not bothered. I'm a sorry fellow without a family. You are now a proper family man. You may have several sisters like this. Go on, go on... Poor girl, that Raani... Let her not know any of this...'

Guruswamy was ascending the stairs of his house, prasadham in hand, listening to this banter. Thinking of Velappan's impishness, he smiled to himself. What did

Ravi know, after all? Guruswamy had known Velappan for several years now. It was astonishing to think how drastically time changed things and how it also erased all traces of such changes.

9

'THAMBIYAPPA, WHY DON'T YOU TEACH THIS BOY something? He knows nothing. I met his teacher from the Malaiyaan school. He had a lot of complaints about the boy. He doesn't even know to count from one to ten! There is a saying in our caste that Nairs may sell leaves for their living but never their dignity. But I'm afraid this boy might be the reason we lose all our dignity!'

The boy who stood holding on to his father, Kesu Nair's, finger, playing with a hibiscus bud nipped from the plant in the yard, was Velappan.

'You little tyke! Come here, don't nip those flowers. Stand here. Is it true what your father says about you? You can't count from one to ten?'

'He is exaggerating, Saamiyappo! I can count from one to hundred straight and backwards from hundred to one. He is blowing things out of proportion. I wanted to go with him to the bazaar. He doesn't want to take me. So, he is telling tales about me. My teacher never said anything about me.'

'Oh, your boy has grown up! Look how he's made you out as a liar!'

'Dei, shall I come to your school and ask your teacher whether or not he complained to me about you yesterday?'

'No worries. You proceed to the bazaar. But what's the need for a provisions broker to go so early to the bazaar?'

'You don't know the half of it, Thambiyappa. Loads of rice and other provisions from Villuppuram, Madurai and Sankarankoil arrive here in the middle of the night. Forwarding agents rush there first and get a sizable portion of everything. We don't have a shop or a godown, do we? So, the earlier I go in the morning, the higher the chances of getting samples of rice, lentils, dried chillies or other grains. If I take it to four or five wholesale shops, I can convince at least two to buy those loads, earning myself a decent commission. Whatever rice or lentils that are left with me from the samples are useful for the day's food.'

'I see, going early reaps you two benefits. Still, I guess there won't be much to save for the future. It is only you and your son at home, isn't it?'

'Yes, what's there to save! I can earn only on Tuesdays and Fridays – the days when the market opens. Even that is unpredictable. Occasionally, there are also market days where I don't earn anything. I can't afford to buy food for this boy from the club every day. His mother was lucky to have passed away so early, not having to witness all these struggles. No creature on earth would have seen the struggles I see every day with this boy. I tell you, Thambiyappa. I'll wait a few more days to see if he improves. All is well if he studies well. If not, I've already had a word with a shopkeeper here. I'll just leave him there to be a servant boy… Let him carry stuff or deliver tea to people, whatever.'

'Vei, Nair! Don't do anything of that sort. He's a good boy. Let him study. It's better if he studies a little and gets a job in some shop, don't you think? Fine, bring him here every morning. I'll look after him. You proceed now.'

After Kesu Nair left, Guruswamy watched the boy carefully. He wore single-stone studs in both ears, had handsome features and a dark skin tone. He looked like a good boy. He was not new to Guruswamy. He lived in the neighbourhood, after all. They crossed paths quite frequently. But now, Guruswamy had taken the responsibility of making sure he studied properly. If not, the boy would be tossed into the world of bazaars and petty shops.

'Velappa!'

'Yes?'

'What did you have in the morning?'

'Nothing yet…'

From the aroma that came from the kitchen, Guruswamy realized that Subbulakshmi was making upma for breakfast.

'Subbu!' he called out aloud.

'What is it? I haven't gotten any work done all morning.' Subbulakshmi came out. Seeing Velappan at the door, she asked, 'How come he's here so early in the morning?'

'Kesu Nair just left him here. He wants me to teach the boy something.'

'Oh, that's grand! Why, does he think the four-rupee rent he pays is excessive? And you, like a generous soul, take up everything!'

'Be quiet, the boy is right there. Have you made coffee and breakfast? Keep some aside for the boy as well.'

'I'm making only upma today. I didn't make any batter for dosa yesterday. Let me finish making breakfast. You do as you please.' Subbulakshmi returned to the kitchen, wiping her face with the free end of her saree.

The memory of that first day with Velappan was fresh in Guruswamy's mind even today. He wished there were a way to burn and destroy old memories just as we burned old objects. Wished there were a way to burn mundane memories, dreams, tastes, pleasures and pains… Chi, what far-fetched things he was wishing for!

How quickly time has fled, thought Guruswamy, even as his memories spread out further. It was a few years after his father had passed away. After his father lived, splurged and left the place, Subbulakshmi had straightened up the surroundings and put together a serene lifestyle for them. Those days that felt like a calm after a storm were still pleasantly etched in his mind.

This same plantation… After all the changes it had gone through, it was still the same plantation. The same majestic naalukkettu house with its wooden beams and tiled roof… After that day when Kesu Nair had left his son under Guruswamy's care, Velappan attended school cursorily and roamed around the neighbourhood the rest of the day. His father had been right – Velappan was not very interested in studies. He stayed at Guruswamy's home all day under the pretext of studying. His father, too, left him to his own devices, trusting Guruswamy to take care of the boy. Amidst all this, Subbulakshmi found Velappan's assistance a big relief. Initially, she chased him away every time he entered the house. But as time passed, she said, 'He's a good boy. Whatever you say, he never speaks a word against you.' He tailed Guruswamy wherever he went. He accompanied Guruswamy to the Padmanaba Swamy Temple every day, and made it a habit to count the temple steps when they went up. Guruswamy never went to see the deepa aaradhanai or the main deity. He always went straight to the inner hall of the temple, which contained various sculptures on the walls and pillars. What he saw in those sculptures every day, Velappan had no idea. Sculptures of women with large breasts carrying lamps in their hands… 'Aiye, shame, shame,' Velappan would cry and run to the priest to get some sandal paste. When he returned, Guruswamy would be standing with his mouth agape in front of a different statue. 'Ammov! Saamiyappa does not worship the deity at the temple. He only watches the statues on the pillars!' Velappan would report gleefully to Subbulakshmi. 'God resides only in those pillars for your Saamiyappa. That's his secret,' she would respond with a smile, throwing a meaningful glance at Guruswamy.

Meanwhile, Guruswamy had not completely given up on the political activism he was known for during his school days. People from the party visited him often at his home. It was the time of corrupt rule in a freshly independent India. Anyone who had the support of a few thugs and a fluent tongue came to the fore. On the other hand, an educated mob functioned solely on the principle that it was their intellectual duty to oppose and criticize whoever was in power. They preferred to stay in their cosy cocoon and cite how developed countries toiled relentlessly and sacrificed many lives to get to where they were. In those days, the crowded Pazhavangaadi Fort grounds – where the two main roads of the town intersected – served as the prime venue for most political gatherings. Hardly a day passed without a political gathering.

Apart from grazing through the sculptures in the temple hall, Velappan accompanied Guruswamy to all the political rallies conducted at the Pazhavangaadi grounds. Although words thrown around in these gatherings – like landowners, the bourgeoisie, peasants and labourers – did not reach the boy, he was amused by the fervent and animated faces of the speakers. But he realized very early that one needed to be quite smart to be able to deliver such an impassioned speech and immediately switch to wearing a broad smile while receiving a garland around the neck. He resolved that he would become a political leader when he grew up.

When he was in fourth grade, Velappan threw a tantrum, saying he did not want to go to school any more. He had gathered a few of his classmates and chanted the slogan, 'Victory be to the revolt,' at school. The headmaster, who was an erstwhile patron of the king and a member of his community party after Independence, asked him to bring his father to school. When things did not improve after that, he put his foot down and expelled Velappan. That was when the boy came weeping to Guruswamy, saying he was not interested in studies. Seeing the bruises made by the headmaster's cane on Velappan's thighs, Kesu Nair also decided that enough was enough. He arranged for Velappan to work as an assistant at one of the commission shops. When the shopkeeper complained that he could not work with a Malayali boy and that he needed someone who knew Tamil, Velappan stopped working there and came to Guruswamy's home. He found company in boys like him from within and around the plantation, learnt to ride a bicycle and roamed around aimlessly. One day, he was found in the company of a few cow herder boys who were taking their buffaloes to the river, which earned him a severe beating from his father.

'Born in a dignified Nair household, and you go around with boys from the Konar caste! I'd rather have you serve at a small tea shop, fetching water. That way, our dignity won't be lost, and we will earn some money as well. If you are so bent on taking buffaloes to bathe in the river and cleaning toilets, I'll wash my hands of you and go my way. I can take care of myself. To think I was glad I had a son… I can handle it if you suck out my life, but don't you dare ruin the family's honour!'

Guruswamy knew of Velappan's new habits and his father's worries. One day, he called Velappan and said, 'Velappa, you are twelve years old. You can't go on like this… I've been watching everything your father is going through. From now on, you are going to be at my home, taking care of the chores here. You don't have to do any menial jobs at a random tea shop like your father wants you to. You can be here until you secure a decent job. We have a cow here. Subbulakshmi is not able to manage it all by herself. You just have to stand there when the milkman comes, collect the milk from him and deliver it to a couple of houses here. I've asked your father not to worry about you any more.'

10

THAT WAS HOW VELAPPAN, SON OF KESU NAIR, BECAME Guruswamy's man. He learnt to speak good Tamil. He became quite fond of Sankaran, the tall milkman. He imitated Sankaran in every way – wearing a baniyan on his torso and a towel around his head like a turban, carrying the milk pots, and walking with a slight limp that Sankaran had because of callused feet. Early every morning, when Sankaran came calling, 'Ammov, I've come to milk the cow,' Velappan would get up immediately and join him. Every person has their own scent. Once you guide them in the direction of their scent, they latch onto it and come up in life. But if you pull them towards a distant dream away from that direction, it only results in regrets and eventually takes them to where they were always supposed to go – like water down a slope. In cases like this, the saying, 'The child is the father of man,' is wrong. With Velappan, he showed no signs as a child. When he accompanied Guruswamy to the political rallies at the Pazhavangaadi ground and later imitated the mannerisms of the speakers, Guruswamy even wondered if Velappan might become a politician some day. In the end, he emerged as a student of the milkman Sankaran.

Velappan always treated Subbulakshmi like his mother. One day, he said, 'Yammov, I will be milking the cow tomorrow at dawn. Sankaran Anna is down with a fever. He says he can't come.' The cow kicked him into the plantains. Even the brass pot he carried that day was dented permanently by that fall.

'Never ever come forward to milk the cow any more. Then your father will come crying to us that we attempted to kill you with our cow. He has already spread the word that we have confined you to the house like a bond slave. He hasn't paid the four-rupee monthly rent in six months now. No one in this household questions him either.'

'Yammov, stay quiet for some time! Oh, what words I have to hear for startling the cow! It didn't not kick me because I'm a stranger. She has a small cut on her left udder. Sankaran Anna had instructed me not to touch that part. I accidentally touched it in the darkness. Now, get me that small pot and see how I milk her now...' Velappan returned to the cow carefully and stroked its face. Then, he stepped closer and patted its back and brushed its lower back affectionately. He brought the calf closer and tied its rope around the backyard pillar. Just as he slowly lowered the pot and squatted near the hind legs of the cow, it shifted its legs restlessly. Alarmed, Velappan backed away hastily.

Subbulakshmi, who was watching all this, burst out laughing.

'If you're so scared, why do you keep approaching her?'

'Yammov, stop laughing,' he said, squatting again. The cow stood calm and still, unaware of the tension it had created only a moment ago. Velappan's first milking duty was at last accomplished successfully.

Even when Sankaran came back to work a couple of days later, Velappan was found coaxing him, saying, 'Let me do it, Anna… I mean, my most respectable teacher…'

Sankaran knew well how to benefit from Velappan's enthusiasm. He replied, 'My dear student, you can't learn everything for free. You have milked the cow when I was ill; I'll let that go. But there are rituals to be done to complete your education. First, you must place a silver coin inside a five-rupee note, roll it in a betel leaf and present it to me. There's more. You also have to gift me a new towel and a dhoti. If you don't do these, the cow won't stay tame. The calf may get diarrhoea. No matter how much you try, the udders won't secrete milk. Mind it. Now, run along and get me a one-aana beedi.'

Gradually, with Sankaran's blessings, Velappan began milking cows at an Iyengar man's house in a brahmin street of Valiyasalai, then at Nallakkannu Chettiyar's house on Kamuku Vilaagam Street whenever Sankaran was unwell or busy. Somehow, Velappan developed a liking for the job. Nairs usually do not usually herd or milk cows. The Pandaris, a lowly subcaste within the Nairs, are the only ones involved in cow trading and dairy products. When Kesu Nair came to know of Velappan's interest in milking cows, he grumbled, 'Son of a Pandari… Let him rot as he wishes. Thambiyappa and his wife have completely ruined him!'

'Ammov! Didn't you use to laugh whenever I picked up the milking vessel earlier? You must see me now Do you know the breed of the cow at the Valiyasalai Iyengar's house? It's a Karachi cross… The size of a small elephant… I milked it single-handedly – a big potful of milk. Do you know what the lady of the house said? 'Dei, aren't you the son of Kesu Nair, the commission broker? You milk so skilfully like a Pandari or a Konaar,' she said!'

Velappan milked cows at daybreak, and then, as the sun rose, he delivered the milk to the neighbouring houses. He bought vegetables every day for Subbulakshmi to cook and helped her in the evenings to grind rice batter. He drew water from the well (there was a flush-out latrine now where the well used to be) and cleaned the stable thoroughly every day. He built a thatched screen around the manure pit where all the cow dung was collected. He made garlands with alternating bands of hibiscus flowers and tulsi leaves every day – some of it for the lamp in the house and the rest for the Devi temple. He watched all the movies that were screened at the Aryasalai cinema talkies. Once, when he narrated the sentimental story of a brother and sister from the movie *Paasamalar*, not only did he shed copious tears, but he also made Subbulakshmi weep.

In fact, Subbulakshmi was averse to movies and drama in general. Knowing that she went to the Chenthitta Devi Temple every Tuesday and Friday, Velappan asked, 'Yemmov, why don't you go watch a movie with Saamiyappa? *Srivalli*, a religious movie featuring Sivaji is running at the talkies. Go and watch it. Saamiyappa will definitely accompany you if you ask him.' He followed it up with an excellent narration of the scenes where Lord Murugan appeared and the scenes between the hunter and the old man.

'Velappa, I'm completely satisfied with your narrations. Why bother going to the crowded talkies where people from all walks gather! We live next to the Devi temple, remember? I'm not so much into movies either. Your Saamiyappa is even worse.'

'You two are so old-fashioned, Ma,' Velappan laughed. 'You must see Padmini, who appears as Valli in that film. She looks exactly like you!'

'Velappa, go, mind your work now.' Subbulakshmi laughed and brushed it aside.

Thanks to the influence of the films he watched, Velappan's gait assumed a new grace. He cropped his hair stylishly with a lock of long hair at the back. The thin moustache that was just sprouting on his face gave it a warm glow. He bought magazines that were rife with images from movies. One day, he framed a picture from the film *Naadodi Mannan* – in which the lead actor M.G.R. posed majestically with a sword in hand – and fixed it on a wall in his house. Irked by this gesture, Kesu Nair complained to Guruswamy, 'I have kept a couple of pictures of deities on that wall. Now, he has sullied the wall with a film poster. He has only grown in age, Thambiyappa. All this is happening right in front of your eyes. Gone are the times when he used to listen to my words. You have to talk to him and correct his ways.'

'Nair, he earns ten or twenty rupees a month by milking cows. At least he's not wasting his time like other boys of his age. Moreover, times have changed. You could go without a meal these days, but you can't skip a movie. Let him be; there's nothing to be worried about.'

Velappan had long wished to buy a wristwatch. So, he never spent even a paise unnecessarily. He gave every extra paise he had to Subbulakshmi, entrusting her with his savings.

When Subbulakshmi was pregnant for the third time, he was beside her all the time, assisting her during every visit to the doctor.

'Please rest now, Ma. I'll grind the spices. Remember, I'm from a respected Nair family.'

'Dei, you are a man, not a child any more. It's not your job to grind spices, light the stove and wash dishes. I'm not so weak that I can't take care of these things. And I have Parvathi for help.'

'But you don't let her inside the kitchen on account of her caste and untidiness. These days, we should measure people only by how clean their heart is.'

'Velu, you talk too much these days. Let Swami not hear you. Now, go and buy the medicines the doctor has prescribed.' Subbulakshmi laughed and sent him on his way.

Irrespective of the time of day or where he was, Velappan rushed to buy medicines for Subbulakshmi.

Since her first two pregnancies had been unsuccessful, the lady doctor had instructed Subbulakshmi to be careful. She was taken to the nursing home one whole month before she was due. It was Velu who walked up and down between the hospital and the house every day. It was he who suffered anxiety bouts, more than Guruswamy or even Subbulakshmi.

But what happened in the end?

Before Guruswamy returned from the blood bank with the required bottles of blood, her breathing had subsided.

Velappan wailed hard, swaying his head like a woman. Despite his own misery, Guruswamy had to console Velappan, which helped alleviate his own pain a little.

'Velu, calm down. Do you think your pain is more than what I feel? Calm down, now…'

'Saamiyappo… I had no awareness when my own mother passed away. But this mother has also left me now, Saamiyappo. She said she would buy me a watch when she was back home after childbirth. My dear mother… She's gone…'

'Are you going to quieten now, or shall I leave?' Guruswamy asked abruptly to make Velappan stop crying.

How quickly days managed to bury past memories!

From dawn through day and dusk to nightfall, wasn't every day the same? Yet, how effortlessly days and memories manage to dry up, wither, turn to dust and disappear! Yesterday's heaviness cannot be found in the heart today. By tomorrow, its intensity will be completely gone until it can be found no more. Every passing day washes over us like a breeze. Perhaps days should be renamed as breeze.

11

WHAT DID SUBBULAKSHMI'S DEMISE DO TO GURUSWAMY'S life? Nothing he set his heart on seemed to stay with him. First, it was Ammu Amma, with her cat-like eyes, soft touch and oil-scented skin. Then, Subbu came after a long time, but she, too, was snatched away. Now he was like a man at the edge of the pond, waiting with his fishing rod immersed in water, watching only the expanse of nothingness in front of him. Why keep up this pretense? If this was a pretense – a mask – what indeed was the true face underneath it? If he asked the question 'What,' all he heard in response were the echoes of the same question, as if pronounced inside a closed cave.

'Guruswamy, how long are you going to live alone like this? Why don't you marry again? It's nothing new in your family. Your grandfather's grandfather had three wives. Your grandfather had two, apart from four or five concubines. Of course, you know how your father was. And I know you very well. It is people who *look* like saints that can't be trusted. You need a marriage, at least on paper. If you have that, no one will mind even if you do something shady outside your household.'

When someone gave him such advice, Guruswamy realized how well they knew him. However, such words could also have strengthened his resolve to remain alone. It was as if he wanted to prove them wrong.

'Velappa, come, let's go to the Pazhavangaadi Temple, and then also visit the Padmanaba Swamy Temple,' he called out as he stepped out of the house. This was his routine. He planted the saplings of his dreams in activities like watching the sculptures in the temples, scrutinizing the lesser-known 'hidden sculptures' on the lower platform of the flagpole at the Srikandeswaram Temple, losing himself in books like *Srungara Rasavallari* (The Book of Romance) and *Maanasa Suthra Rahasyam* (The Secrets of the Heart). He forgot all his burdens in the vagaries of life.

Meanwhile, Velappan had secured a permanent job. His job was to milk the cows in the large dairy farm of Paalai Arunachalam, whose family had been in the dairy business for generations. It was a busy space, where several men took care of anywhere between ten and thirty cows and milked them every morning and evening. They also owned a depot at the market, through which they sold milk, butter, curd and ghee. Made from undiluted milk, their butter had the consistency of wax and was usually sold out before seven in the evening. Anyone who wanted to procure butter after that had to wait until the next morning. Their milk was, likewise, undiluted. The Municipal Corporation food inspectors tried their best to find something off with Paalai Arunachalam's dairy products, but they found not an iota of evidence of adulteration.

Paalai Arunachalam had a large family – five sons and three daughters. All of them had gone to college and completed a B.A. or M.A. degree. The eldest son had become the manager of the depot soon after he finished his studies. A name plate announcing 'Manager Vaageesa Dass, B.A. (Hons.)' was fixed above the cushioned chair he occupied at the depot. He looked majestic, with fair sandalwood complexion, slightly balding and a small paunch, wearing a loose full-sleeved white kurta, gold chain, wristwatch and a large ring on his finger. Everything at the depot was handled hygienically, with parchment papers, clean bottles, and sealed packing. The fragrance of expensive incense sticks – not the odour of butter or curd – welcomed anyone who entered the place. Even in those days, apart from a couple of large wholesale shops, the police station and the post office, the depot was the only place that had a telephone. The depot was so popular that securing a job there was like being employed by the government.

'Oh, you work at the milk farm! Then it must be easy for you to find a girl from an upper-class family,' was how people generally reacted when they learnt someone worked at the depot.

It was when Velappan was helping Guruswamy with odd jobs and errands after Subbulakshmi's death that Guruswamy pulled some strings and got him this job. Vaageesa Dass and Guruswamy had studied together at school.

One day, when Guruswamy was crossing the veterinary hospital on his way back from his morning walk, Vaageesa Dass stopped his car and got out. They had been chatting for a while when Guruswamy said in passing, 'There's a boy working at the grove… An expert in milking cows… He's born a Nair, but even Konar men can't hold a candle to him.'

'Guru, what's there for me to say when you speak so highly of him? Ask the boy to come and meet me one day.'

True to his word, when Velappan went to meet him, Dass agreed to employ him immediately.

'Come to work at an auspicious hour tomorrow. Let's

get you started with the evening shift of milking,' Dass had said.

Paalai Arunachalam, the father, was, however, not pleased with this.

'Dass, what's this you have done? You've sent a little boy to work at the farm. That, too, a Nair boy… They may look meek, but they are such a conceited bunch. Look at the boy! He'll fly away if our cows sigh deeply!' Arunachalam grumbled to Vaageesa Dass.

'Appa, it's going to be difficult to extract work out of these old Konaar men we have now. We need to hire young boys and men who are ready to put in the effort. In fact, we need to change the way they look. There must be a unique identity to employees of the depot,' Dass responded hotly.

Paalai Arunachalam had taken a back seat by then. His sons were taking care of everything. He had his own Hillman car and a driver for it. He went to the beach and the Padmanaba Swamy Temple every evening before returning to his bungalow. After all, when he had able sons to take care of things, what worry did he have in life?

When Velappan earned a salary of thirty rupees for his first month's work, he came straight to Guruswamy, placed the money at his feet and fell at his feet in reverence.

'Dei, Velappa, what's this foolishness? Get up now.

Acting like a fool… There's at least some use if you fell at Devi's feet in the temple. What has happened now?'

'You showed me the way to learn something. Now, I've earned a solid amount for the first time using the skill. Here…' Velappan said, rising to his feet and handing over the money to Guruswamy.

'As if I showed you a glorious way. Now go, give the money to your father. Poor man, he's been struggling for some time now. Imagine how happy he'll be to see this money! He has also grown old now. Ask him to stay at home. Don't let him walk up and down to the bazaar any more. This salary should suffice for the two of you going forward.'

'Saamiyappo, I totally forgot to tell you. It's been three days since Appa left the house. No clue as to why or where he went. I wake up at around four in the morning and go to work. After milking the cows in the morning, I accompany the boys who take the cows to the river for bathing. By the time that's done and I come home, Appa would have left for work. I go again for milking in the evening, then catch a movie at the cinemas and come home to sleep on the outside porch. I didn't even notice anything unusual. It was only on the second day that I realized there was not a sound from inside the house. He usually coughs frequently when he's asleep. Suspecting something was off, I opened the door and found him missing. I went to the bazaar yesterday afternoon and enquired at the usual places. They asked me about Appa's whereabouts in return! What could I tell them? I thought he might have gone somewhere nearby. But there has been no news about him, and it's been three days!'

'Oh god! So much has happened, and it's been three days? You couldn't find time to inform me about this? Are you that busy with your new job? Let it be… Did you ask Parvathi or Pappan? They might know something.'

'No one seems to know anything. Even Pappan Anna asked me if Father is out of town, visiting someone. I couldn't tell him anything. You're the only one I've told about this.'

'Where could he have gone? Maybe to visit some relatives of yours?'

'Who do we have? I had a cousin at Maavelikkarai, but she died last year. There are also other relatives here… Near Kuriyathi… But he has never visited any of them. You know how stubborn he is, Saamiyappa. You know how cross he was with me after I became a part of your household. It is only recently that he began speaking to me normally again.'

'That's true… Did he fight with you recently? Not necessarily in the past week, but did he?'

'Saamiyappo, trust me. I swear in the name of Devi, we didn't fight.'

'You don't have to invoke Devi's name for these things. Anyway, let me enquire at the bazaar. Perhaps he went to Kollam or Kottayam with a client?'

'Impossible! There's no one like that. You know him. He never liked to go to any place outside our Chaalai. Hmm, where could he have gone? He'll surely come back. Of all days, he's gone missing just when I earned my first salary! Anyway, I'll start for the evening shift of milking. Saamiyappo, ask around about my father at the bazaar when you go to the temple later today.'

'Yes, you go ahead. What other job do I have? I'll skip Srikandeswaram Temple today. I'll visit Sabapathi Temple and check about your father at the bazaar. Given his personality, he wouldn't have gone anywhere. He has never been comfortable with faking a smile and holding a conversation with anyone. Oh, the time is two already. Get going, then. I'll see what I can do...'

Despite these consolations, Kesu Nair was not to be found that day, the next day, the next month or even the next year. He had gone without leaving a clue behind. The man who proudly repeated that 'a good Nair may sell leaves for their living but never their dignity' had disappeared without a word. A missing-person complaint was filed at the police station, but nothing came of it. Guruswamy was perplexed by the whole affair whenever he thought about it. Who knew the dizzying depths that a man's stubbornness could take him to?

'There was an elderly man in our clan who fought with his wife and left the house. He came back after fourteen years, like Lord Rama returned from the forest, with a long beard and matted hair. What happened after that? They even had a couple of kids after that!' Vengu Bhagavathar recounted a story whenever talk of Kesu Nair came up.

If someone asked Velappan if he had not looked for his father, he would respond curtly, 'I've looked for him wherever I can. I'm also worried about what could have happened to the old man. But can I also give up on my life for that?'

The matter was discussed no more.

12

'SAAMIYAPPO!'

'Dei, Velappa, what's going on? Your moustache and hairstyle are getting fancier by the day, I see. What were you hollering my name for?'

'Nothing. I've been meaning to talk to you about something for a few days now. I come here, see your face, get nervous and leave. But I've made up my mind to talk to you today. Who else do I have, anyway? You are the only one to whom I can talk about it...'

'Do you know who you remind me of now? That actor Sivaji Ganesan, who appears in the films you watch... What with that moustache and hairstyle... You have indeed grown up!'

'How do you know about it, Saamiyappo?'

'Dei, I can't make head or tail of what you're saying these days. How do I know about what?'

'No... It's just that Raani – the girl at the milk farm – also says the same thing about me.'

'What does she say?'

'That I look like Sivaji.'

'The sister of the farm's proprietor talks to you so casually and treats you with respect? What's going on, Velappan Nair? Tell me more...'

'Oh, she speaks to me very freely. She mocks me a lot. God, she's so talkative. The moment she sees me, she starts chatting about films. 'I've watched *Ambikapathi*, the new film that was released recently. Do you like Padmini or Savithri more?' and on and on... I swear on you, Saamiyappa, initially, I struggled to find words to talk to her. Early in the morning, she used to come and stand next to me at the cowshed. Even the maids around there looked at us suspiciously. I felt awkward and self-conscious, but she never seemed to mind. One morning, when she was standing close to me and teasing me, Dass came out of the house with his toothbrush in hand. He saw us and asked what was happening. 'Look at this Velappan... I ask him to fill this vessel for me with some fresh milk, and he has the nerve to refuse!' she complained to him. 'Velappa, she's an adamant girl. Give her what she wants,' he said and left. And here she was, laughing her head off. Such a mischievous girl!'

'You bold imp! Looks like you've lost your heart to her... Tell me, what else has happened?'

One day, when she was teasing me as usual, she suddenly asked me what my age was. I told her I'm twenty-two. 'It's time for you to get married then,' she said. I said, 'There's no rush for me to get married. But you must also be over twenty now… I should talk to your father and ask him to start looking for a groom for you. Shall I talk to Dass sir, your brother?'

'Oh, go ahead. If you're so courageous, ask my brother to marry me off to you if you can,' she retorted, and it took my breath away for a moment. 'Shocked, are you? That's how I'm going to plainly ask my brother,' she said and laughed merrily like a child. She didn't seem to have any idea of what she was saying or who she was talking to… The other day, I had gone to the cinemas at night to watch the film *Devadasu*, which was re-released then. As fate would have it, Raani came to the same theatre with a huge group that day. She, her two elder brothers, the elder sister who's been married off in Mettur, the other sister whose name is Chairanthridevi, their children… All of them occupied the balcony of the theatre. When I stepped out during the intermission, Raani spotted me, summoned me and bought me a coffee. Then she turned towards her sister and said, 'This is Velappan… Works on our farm. A gem of a man. Doesn't miss a single movie.' Then she invited me to the balcony to watch the film with them. I didn't know how to turn down her invitation. Even her sister invited me without a second thought, and I went along. There was only one empty seat there, and it was next to Raani's. They are educated people, and they showed no sign of embarrassment or discomfort! I sat there gingerly, acutely conscious of my position. Aiyo, Saamiyappa… The moment the movie began playing, she began chatting with me about the film, narrating scenes so casually like she does with her sister. She even pinched my arm a couple of times… Can a girl be any more mischievous! You know what? She comes to me at the cowshed the next morning and says, 'Velu Nair did not let me watch the film in peace last night.' I knew she was teasing me, but the lie still irked me. I told her bluntly not to go around talking like that. She's been taunting me more than ever since then. Her laughter and her mockery… These days, it bothers me only if she doesn't tease me. It disturbs me so much that I can't even fall asleep on such days…'

'I see… Things have gone that far, eh? And you're narrating it so coolly to me! You're a grown man already… A twenty-two-year-old donkey… Hmm… Don't step too deep into it and ruin the job you have. More importantly, don't you injure my reputation! I asked you for more and more details only to see how far things have gone. Dei, rascal! Let's forget what you told me. Had we kept you in your place, things wouldn't have gone this far.'

Velappan stood quietly, head bowed. Was he weeping? He was a grown man now, and yet he had so much respect for Guruswamy. *Poor boy, he's a good fellow,* thought Guruswamy.

'Saamiyappa, do you really mean it? Would Subbu Amma have agreed with you? I don't have anyone to call my own now. I don't even remember my mother. The mother who brought me up is no more. My father was almost a non-presence in my life… Even when he was around, his presence made no difference. You are the one person who has known me from when I was a little boy… You have been with me all along, helped me grow up and become what I am today. I believed you were that one soul who knew my heart really well… It's all gone now…'

'Dei, stop it! Stop crying now. You've learnt good Tamil and cloying lines from all those movies you watch! All right, tell me… What does Raani want? Do you think this is child's play? You know their status and where she belongs. Does she now know the seriousness of what she's saying?'

Velappan immediately produced a rolled-up piece of paper from the folds of his dhoti, handed it to Guruswamy and hurried down the stairs.

To my dear Velappan,

I can't handle this any more. You can't continue being a coward. My father and brother are on the verge of fixing a groom for me from Sengottai. How can you stay quiet even now? I'm waiting for your word... If you just show the sign, I'm ready to run away with you wherever it is you decide in the blink of an eye. I don't care for all this wealth or status. I want to live with you. So, please make up your mind quickly... I don't know what more to say. Even as I write this, my thoughts keep coming around to you. Since I'm used to teasing you so much, it has become harder for me to openly tell you how I feel about you. I can't handle this any more. Please respond at the earliest.

With love,

Raani.

It was only after reading the letter that Guruswamy understood the gravity of the situation. *Oh, he's gone too deep into it,* he thought and raised his head from the letter to find the rascal back in front of him again.

'Have you read it, Saamiyappo?'

Guruswamy glared at Velappan, whose eyes were already brimming with tears. His face had reddened, and his lips were quivering, as if he was going to burst out crying anytime now.

'What's the use of tears now? Things have gone too far now. Tell me, what are you going to tell her? She's written an impassioned letter on the glory of her love. How are you going to answer her?'

Velappan burst into tears.

'Saamiyappo, I don't know what to do…' Tears streamed from his eyes continuously.

'I'll talk to Dass and ask him to find a good groom for her. Idiot, he was the same even during our school days. The men in his family had their eyes trained only on making money. Chairanthri, the eldest daughter in their family, was twenty-eight or thirty by the time they realized she needed to be married off! Looks like they're still focused on elevating their status and accumulating wealth… Where has it led to? This girl has lost her mind while they were looking the other way. I'll talk to Dass today and set things in motion.'

'Saamiyappo?'

'What is it?'

'When you set things in motion, please let it be a favourable one…'

'Are you out of your mind? Do you realize what you're saying? Have you also lost your senses like that girl?'

'Yes!'

'Yes, he says!'

Velu wiped his eyes dry and stood erect.

'I love her, too…'

Guruswamy was startled by his response.

She's from an affluent family. A spoiled girl, even. What does she know about the consequences of her desires? She's watched a lot of movies and read a lot of magazines… Fascinated by the love stories in them, she's floating in her own imagination. She has grown up in a confined, wealthy space outside of which she knows nothing. But he must know better! Legendary love stories like that of Ambikapathy and Amaravathy are not practical in today's world. He knows nothing about Dass's family. How dare he say he loves her, too! Unlike their father, Dass and his brothers treat their employees better. They are kind even to the lowliest of their servants. It has led him to take advantage of their kindness and fall in love with their sister… But their family is so influential that they could eliminate him without a trace of his existence. Giving this boy some liberty has landed him in great danger now. What can be done?

'Velappa! Did you think about who you are before speaking your mind? Compare yourself with that family.

I'm not even talking about your clan here. It's become common for Malayali men to marry Tamil girls these days. But do you realize what kind of family theirs is? Are you in any way comparable to them? Do you think it's a task like milking a cow the day after it has given birth to a calf? Their family is like a temple cow. It's not for ordinary people to touch, let alone try to milk. You better quit that job and come back. She's a naive girl living in her own fantasies. I'll talk to Dass and ask him to arrange a marriage for Raani soon. Looks like you may get me into trouble.'

'Saamiyappo!'

'What more do you have to say?'

'The two of us have decided. If you've also given up on us, our corpses will be floating in the temple pond tomorrow morning.'

'Oh, you showed me this letter only after having discussed and made a decision, is it?'

'I showed you the letter because I didn't know how I could explain our situation to you…'

'Hmm, if things have progressed that far, then there's no option but for the two of you to jump into the temple pond,' Guruswamy said abruptly before going into the pooja room and shutting the door behind him.

Velappan sat there and waited for a long time. Then he left the house, thinking, *Let him come out whenever he calms down.*

The moment Velappan left, Guruswamy came out of the room with a beatific smile.

13

ONE AUSPICIOUS MORNING, VELAPPAN MARRIED RAANI BY tying the holy thread around her neck at the Devi temple premises. The only other witnesses were the gentle breeze, the still-dark morning sky, the single lamp that was alight in the temple and Parvathi, who sat on the temple pial blinking cluelessly.

'Velappa, don't delay further. The bus to Nagercoil will be the first one at the Thampanoor terminus. It'll start before five in the morning. Do you have the reserved ticket safe with you? There are several buses from Nagercoil to Madurai. Remember everything I've told you. And, Raaniyamma… You're an educated girl. Don't get carried away by the joyous moment; be careful. Act sensibly and wisely. Your father and brothers will definitely gather a bunch of men to look for the two of you. What's the worst they can do to me? I'll handle it all. I have no fear as long as I have Devi's blessings. Hmm… Pray to her and get going. Pappan is waiting outside. He'll accompany you until the bus terminus. Hurry up... If someone has already realized Raani is missing at home, this is the first place they'll come to. After all, didn't you say her family was already suspicious about the two of you?'

Even as Guruswamy was giving them instructions, Raani and Velappan fell at his feet.

'Dei, this is no time for these formalities. I asked you to pray to Devi and start immediately. Come on, Raaniyamma. It is your responsibility now to transform this fool into a decent man. Wipe your tears. Everything will be fine. Our Devi will guide us all the way... Aiyaiyo, the rooster is crowing. It's getting late; start already!'

When Velappan and Raani exited the temple as a newly married couple and stepped into the street, Vengu and Pappan were waiting outside, ready to accompany them to the terminus.

'Hurry up, it's four-thirty already,' whispered Vengu.

Guruswamy stood transfixed at the temple and remained so even when Parvathi came to inform him that the couple had crossed Kamuku Vilaagam Street.

What gave me the courage to act like this? I have played a key role in tarnishing the good name of that affluent family. How am I going to face Dass when he eventually comes to enquire about his sister? Did I agree to help them in order to stand by a pure form of love? What purity? I could've at least discussed this matter with Dass, but I didn't. Instead, I helped the naive girl and the foolish boy to get married and run away. And now, here I stand, at the Devi temple, head held high, as if I've accomplished something great. What perversity! Perhaps the whole episode is my way of displaying my perversity? No, it can't be... Yes, it is...

The noise of barking dogs tore through the quiet morning and pulled him out of his thoughts. The sound of the Suprabatham floated down from the speakers at the Aryasalai Temple.

'Saami, the lamp has run out of oil. Shall I extinguish it before it goes off by itself?' Parvathi asked.

'Yes, put it off before you leave. Let it not die on its own without oil,' Guruswamy responded to her absent-mindedly as he climbed the stairs to his house. The sun was rising by then.

Velappan and Raani remained in hiding for about a month. The powerful family that Raani's was, they managed to discover the couple at a lodge in Madurai. When a complaint was filed against Velappan for abducting their girl along with several items of expensive jewellery, the court ruled in Velappan's favour, citing that Raani was a major, and she had the right to choose her spouse.

'Good riddance to her. We'll forget that we had such a girl at our home!' Dass and his family cut ties with her in an attempt to salvage their pride and preserve their family name and wealth.

'Guruswamy – that bearded traitor – is the man behind all this. He lives in Chaalai, and he has a handful of henchmen for support. That's what gives him the nerve to pull off something like this. None of this could have happened without his knowledge. Velappan could not have enjoyed a month-long, safe honeymoon at Madurai without the backing of someone like him. And the villain still resides in Chaalai. I may belong to the Tamil clan, but I was born in this land. I'll teach him a lesson,' grumbled Dass.

One day, two dozen men from Valliyur and Aralvaaimozhi came to Guruswamy's grove, armed with spears and poles, yelling, 'Where's that bogus monk?'

Pappan slipped through the barbed wire fence on the south end of the grove and ran to Chaalai Bazaar. He informed the employees' union office and the party office of the sudden development.

'Henchmen from outside have entered the plantation, threatening to slay our Saami. Come immediately,' he called out.

Within a few minutes, a crowd had gathered at the

main intersection of the bazaar, with daggers, sickles and poles in hand. Thankfully, someone had called the cops by then. The arrival of a huge police force prevented the situation from turning into bloodshed.

'Oh, the dairy farmer has the gall to send men to kill me? From now on, the Nair boy and his new wife are going to stay at his old residence within this grove of mine. Let's see what anyone can do about it,' Guruswamy retorted and promptly sent word to Madurai to bring Velappan and Raani back home.

The newly-weds's fresh start at Guruswamy's plantation gained a celebratory spirit. Although it was obvious that Guruswamy was the mastermind behind everything, no one knew how he made it all possible. Nobody caught him meeting someone or arranging for any of these events to happen.

At times, people even came to Guruswamy himself to lament about the incident: 'Swamy, I heard that your man Velappan has eloped with the girl from the farm? How sad! It is your reputation that is sullied because of that traitor! That ingrate...'

Guruswamy never paid heed to any of this. He would go to his terrace with a gentle smile and assume his usual serene pose. He would remain standing there until the brahminy kite arrived at its customary spot on the tree in the distance. His eyes would widen with curiosity as soon as the kite arrived. He would then go inside his house. The next morning, when Parvathi was busy cleaning the front yard of the house or washing dishes, Guruswamy would come out and meditate under the rays of the rising sun. Or he would gaze at the paintings on the walls of the Devi temple.

Time indeed plays a variety of games in the span of one's life... Raani is the mother of a baby boy, and even the paandu sutthu is done now. The artist, Ravi, is pulling Velappan's leg for flirting with a girl. When a stone is thrown into a pond, the green moss on the surface of the water scatters momentarily, and by the time the stone sinks to the bottom, the moss covers the surface again. People often use this metaphor when it comes to interest in women. Was Velappan demonstrating this trait now? Was he going astray now that Raani had given birth to a baby? Why did it bother Guruswamy so much? When Guruswamy stepped out of his pooja room after spending several minutes in deep meditation and eventually came to the terrace, he found Ravi sitting on the temple's pial and staring at the paintings on the walls as if he was seeing them for the first time.

14

HOW BEAUTIFULLY NATURE DISPLAYED ITS RICHES THROUGH the green leaves of the coconut trees when the rainy season began! Wasn't every season of this Malayala land a different kind of radiant smile?

> When the misty season is here
> Flowers abound on mango trees
> When the snow lifts and summer comes
> 'Tis the season of mango fruits
> After summer, it's time for the rains
> What else, but gushing streams!

Words won't suffice to appreciate the Malayali poet who so succinctly captured the beauty of this land. Every person in this land and every event was poetic indeed. Men like stags, women like swans and a serenity of atmosphere like that of white clouds!

Guruswamy sat on a stool, savouring the fine drizzle

carried by the gentle breeze, which flowed with an intensity somewhere between a chatter and a howl. Opposite him, Ravi was busy observing the contours of Guruswamy's face and painting strokes on the white canvas with his brush.

Guruswamy's heart was leaping with joy, just as the branches of the mango tree danced in the drizzle, shedding droplets so that they could accept more. He could sit there forever, enjoying the scenery. He could see the swaying branches of the mango tree and the coconut trees behind it and the tall maple further behind it. The maple stood like a mighty elephant, swaying lightly in the rain-laden breeze. Where did the brahminy kite that usually perched on the tree go during this season? Was it also enjoying this weather from a distant, rocky abode, having pleasant dreams?

The gentle drizzle turned into a downpour in the blink of an eye. Even the leaves of the mango tree looked like pelting droplets of rain at that moment.

The mango tree belonged to the grove in Guruswamy's father's time. It now stood beyond the stone wall, brushing against the parapet wall of Sait's house. This land was full of fruit-bearing trees like coconut, plantain, jackfruit and tamarind. There also used to be a couple of tall kaanjiram trees here and even a sandalwood tree on the east end of the land. When the first showers arrived after summer, the whole grove – including the grass, shrubs and trees – turned green immediately, as if they had been waiting for it all along. The bamboos and the touch-me-nots in the grove bloomed green and smiled like newborn children in this season. It was very common to spot Indian rat snakes slither away from the foot-high undergrowth when people squatted near the bushes to relieve themselves. A few days into their marriage, when Subbulakshmi had gone to take a shower in the bathroom in their backyard, she had seen two snakes entwined and rolling on the floor. He remembered how he had embraced her when she came in shivering and how they had ended up in bed – she, with her hair oiled before her shower and he, still in the grip of newly-wed bliss… On another occasion, when the Devi temple was opened in the morning, there had been a brown snake entwined around the chain of the hanging lamp. The priest then was an elderly man. He had shouted out, 'Amma,' and had stood there shaking from head to toe, the bell he held in his hand announcing his fear to everyone. The snake had slowly slid down and wound its way through an opening in the wall behind the Devi's statue.

The memories of the greenery and those snakes remained like scars that could now only be felt with blind fingers. The trees were no more. There were a few coconut trees left. There was a hill mango tree and a kapok tree... Just one each. When Chaalai became a town, everything disappeared, washed away by the flood of development. Every street of Kamuku Vilaagam, every alley in Paattu Vilaagam and all paths around the grove were occupied by noisy timber shops and scrap shops that accumulated old tin articles and bottles. Amidst all this, the vestiges of any greenery of the past were hard to find any more.

How effortless it was to recollect all this! Even as Guruswamy thought how clear his mind was, a scornful smile appeared on his face and remained there like a kite hovering high above his mind space.

Anantharangam, his father, had enjoyed a self-indulgent life with money, women and servants. Only a royal man could have owned such vast acres of land and a palatial house in Chaalai. Guruswamy began his primary education in English, which was a luxury in those times. However, what got off to a flying start soon plateaued. In his seventh grade, he experienced his first love. She was a curly-haired, round-faced girl from his class. He went to school regularly, at least to see Sugantha. She never spoke to him or acknowledged his presence with a smile. Once, when he had gone to the beach to witness the king's procession, Sugantha had come there with her father. He was a majestic man with a thick moustache and wore an ornately decorated fez hat, a full coat and a bright white dhoti. 'Acha, this boy studies in my class,' she called to her father and stood beside him with a smile. When her father asked him where he lived and who his father was, there was a hint of guardedness in his voice. The next day at school, she was back to being her usual quiet self, showing no hints of the smile she had given him only the day before. Although he was perplexed by this 'attitude of girls', he nevertheless indulged in several fantasies. He experienced the same kind of glee in those fantasies that he felt when Ammu Amme sang 'Aambaadi thannil ore unniyundangane…'

'Sugantha and I are in love. I had been to her house even yesterday. Her mother greeted me with tea. She also served delicious jackfruit crisps fried in coconut oil. I refused to have the banana upperi. Sugantha and I did our homework together. She even applied henna on my fingers. See how red it has become?' He shared several such imaginary tales with his close friends.

His friends sometimes asked him, 'Dei, Guru, you say Sugantha is your lover. But she never even smiles at you in class?'

'That's how we've resolved to keep this a secret. We've agreed not to let anyone know how close we are,' he responded solemnly.

In those days, his fantasies were enough to keep his imaginary love afloat.

15

THAT WAS WHEN HIS FATHER BOUGHT A GRAMOPHONE BOX. As far as he remembered, there was no other house in Chaalai that possessed a gramophone then. Whenever there was a special occasion like a wedding at a neighbour's or a relative's house, the gramophone was invariably borrowed, and Guruswamy went along with it. What an exhilarating feat it used to be to go through the records, read their labels before picking one, set it on the turntable, wind it and gently place the needle on the disc so that music flowed out of it! Girls and boys of his age looked at him with fascination and envy. Smaller children used to gather around the speaker and wonder who sang from inside the machine. On such occasions, Guruswamy wished Sugantha were there to see him.

He fell into fantasies where Sugantha was Shakuntala and he was King Dushyanta, a romantic pair for which G.N.B. and M.S. had sung a fitting duet. The songs of that age stayed in his heart even after the time had erased much else from his memory. 'Jagannadha Jagannadha…' His heart swelled recollecting the song, like casuarina trees swaying merrily in a drizzly breeze. '… Oh, dear friend, His eyes met mine in the garden where bees swarm, and stole my heart…'

'Like a worm on bait, like a lamp aflame, my heart has suffered for long, oh friend!'… Songs, sweet songs…

Those singers gave poetic shape to the love that blossomed in his heart at such a young age. His father had the discs of all songs from the film *Sri Valli*. 'The bees sing sweet melodies around colourful blossoms…' in Mahalingam's voice, and 'Oh, you lady who wanders these evergreen forests…' in Kittappa's voice were still etched in his heart.

Could one live lost in music, singing songs and raagas without any worries? He had trained his voice a little by singing along with the records. And he had cherished a desire to learn music properly. When he expressed it to his father, it was arranged that he would attend music classes every evening with a tall brahmin lady at the agraharam. Contrary to what he had imagined, he was not allowed to take off with the complicated but wonderful 'Sangeetha Sowbhagyame'. For several weeks, he repeated the same notes… Sa, Re, Ga, Ma, Pa,

Da, Ni, Sa… Notebooks were exhausted, but he moved no further from there. After three arduous months, by the time he tentatively began singing 'Punnai maratthadiyil naangal pagadaigal aadumbodhu…' and 'Thaaye Yadhodha…' he had lost interest in it. The teacher's betel-reddened mouth, her songs and her methods did not suit him. When he erred while singing, she pinched him hard on his thighs. He did not want to continue being tormented by a mere woman – a woman who could not even teach music to an interested pupil. His music classes ended there, but his desire to sing remained unquenched.

The first question he asked Subbulakshmi on the night of their wedding was if she could sing. He smiled, remembering how she had blinked at him cluelessly in response on that dimly lit night.

'I asked if you know how to sing…'

'Um hmm, no…' she mumbled and shook her head.

'What else do you know? Gossip? All women in Parvathipuram seem to know only that.'

She turned her head swiftly and glared at him.

'Oh, you know so many women at Parvathipuram?'

He had not expected that.

'Why? Looks like knowing you is enough to know about them all!' he responded slowly.

When he gripped her shoulder and turned her around to see her face, she was in tears.

Then, it was time to surrender.

'I asked something silly, and you said something silly in response. I snapped… Let's forget it…'

'I lost it when you spoke ill of my place… Sorry…' She fell to his feet in a gesture of apology.

'Ada, this is not such a big thing. Come, now… I'll sing something…'

She laughed. When he tickled her, she laughed even more. When his finger brushed against her skin, she shyly moved a little further.

'Chi, I know how roguish you can get,' she said demurely.

'What do you know?'

'Nothing.'

'Now, that's better. You know nothing, do you? Let me teach you…'

That night, they had let the lamp glow until dawn.

'The lamp has been alight all night…'

'How can you learn in darkness, then?'

She laughed coyly before she left the room.

There had been no songs that night. But he remembered every note he touched that night. Subbulakshmi was a beautiful, shapely veena, with strings that were sensitive to the slightest touch. Calm like a song composed in a low note, she was like a pleasant arrangement of musical notes. She was soft and soothing. Were there traces of Ammu Ammai and Sugantha in his memories of her?

Music followed him at every juncture, be it in those few years of married life with Subbulakshmi, in his father's demise, in those helpless hours he waited outside the maternity ward where Subbulakshmi was struggling with prenatal contractions, in the memories of the faceless infants they had lost after birth, in her ultimate death, in the image of the grove that extended in front of him and even in the empty stare of the kite that perched on that lonely tree. Music pervaded everything like a whiff of breeze that gradually grew stronger and wilder.

His father's days were numbered. Guru's schooling and education had already become a thing of the past by then. His father was intent on getting him married as soon as he turned twenty. That was how Subbulakshmi became his wife.

'Lakshmi… He's a good boy but a wastrel. Take good care of him,' he had said before he passed away.

Guruswamy often wondered in what sense he was a wastrel. He did not have his father's weakness for women. The image of his father and Ammu Ammai in bed had sown in him a strong distaste. Even those dreams he had enjoyed of Sugantha were at an innocent age, untouched by carnal desires. His schooling ended when he was sixteen. That was when Sait bought the western half of their plantation, cut off all the trees and built a bungalow. The other half had remained as it always was, with a few trees and thatched huts. After his schooling, Guruswamy's interests were completely occupied by the temple car festivals, the food festival at Padmanaba Swamy Temple, routine prayers and the nationalist movement that had risen against the monarchy. However, unlike his forefathers, he did not seek wives and concubines. What made Guruswamy a wastrel in his father's eyes was his nationalist chants, khadi attire and the poor company he kept with people of lower classes.

'Your father called you a wastrel. Why, do you visit other women?' Subbulakshmi asked him one night, a few days into their marriage.

He had not responded immediately. He had lain in bed for a few hours, unable to sleep. Then he had woken up Subbulakshmi, who was by then fast asleep, and poured his heart out to her. The lullabies of Ammu Ammai, the horror of seeing her naked on his father's bed, the subsequent revulsion that had settled in him since then, the childhood crush he had on Sugantha and the empty dreams he had woven around her.

'Subbulakshmi, these are my only encounters with women so far. But I can assure you, I'm capable of sensuality beyond your imagination. Come here…' he had said, pulling her for fresh lessons on intercourse. That night had been particularly long for both of them. He demonstrated to her his artful practice of sensuality that night.

'I believe in your ability… Let's sleep now…' Subbulakshmi had gasped at last, conceding defeat, and hushed him to sleep.

After all those empty years since Subbulakshmi's passing, what was in his mind today? Was it the hazy light of a new sun rising in his skies?

PART II

1

THE DAY BROKE WITH CLEAR BLUE SKIES. THE TREE BRANCHES were glowing green, as if washed clean by the rains, and the coconut leaves danced like unsheathed swords in the air. There was a bird crying sharply somewhere – peep… peep… peep – living through its voice. A gentle breeze drifted in, spreading the warmth of the sunshine. Would the kite on that tall tree be facing the other way? A colourful checkered saree was hung to dry on the clothesline tied between the coconut tree in the yard and the roof of the hut. The chants of a procession could be heard from the distant road.

These were changing times. There were chants and cries every other day, fighting for some rights or the other. 'Inquilab Zindabad… Long live the revolution…' People were changing rapidly, too. And yet, this artist named Ravi, who lived inside the plantation, was painting Guruswamy's portrait tirelessly. At a time when cameras could capture one's image perfectly in a click, loyal people like Ravi were hard to come by. He was not sure if even Velappan, Vengu, Pappan and Parvathi were so loyal. Why did he feel so? It was true that Velappan had come to him as a child and grown in his shadow. Now that he was a completely grown man with a wife and a child, was he drifting away?

Shrugging away these thoughts, Guruswamy turned towards Ravi and asked, 'What is it, Ravi? Is it a procession? Do you hear it?'

Ravi looked at Guruswamy in awe, uttering no response.

'Saami, I've troubled you the past five or six days. But it has yielded good results. There's not much left; I'll complete your portrait soon,' he said, wiping his hands.

'How long has it been since you started painting this, Ravi?'

'Don't you remember, Saami? What's gotten into you? I've been noticing these past few days… Sometimes you smile to yourself, sometimes your expression changes suddenly, and occasionally, you even hum under your breath. You are such a strange fellow, Saami… I began painting last Wednesday. It's Tuesday today. Your work is over now. I'll take the board home today. Two more days, and I'll be done. You'll witness your true majesty then. We should find an auspicious day to unveil the portrait in your living room.'

'What's the need for all that? You wanted to paint my portrait. I'm not a monk. I wished to see how you would turn me into a painting. I sat for these sessions only to watch that happen. For the whole of the past week, I was lost in myself. That's perhaps why I even lost count of the days…'

Parvathi came up the stairs with a broom in hand. Guruswamy looked at her eagerly as if he had been away all these days and was seeing her after a long break.

'Yes, Parvathi… You proceed with your work. I'll be downstairs,' he said, rising to his feet.

'Oh Devi! Saami is back to his original self at last! We were cursing this artist all these days. Wait here; Velu, Pappan, and Bhagavathar are downstairs… I'll go tell them the message,' she said, setting her broom down.

'Wait, I'm headed downstairs anyway. If the temple is open, I'd like to go for a prayer. Ravi, come along,' Guruswamy said, turning to Ravi.

'Let's go. I have to take my painting accessories home as well. I need to wash my face and arms, too,' Ravi said, following Guruswamy down the steps, and then headed north towards his house.

Velappan, Vengu and Pappan were seated in the temple yard, playing 'lambs and tigers'. When Guruswamy entered the yard, they rose in a hurry.

Raani, who had just stepped out of the house with her child in her arms, asked Guruswamy teasingly, 'Saamiyappo! Are you out of the trance you've been in for the past five or six days? Or are you sleepwalking?'

She was bright now after the pregnancy, having gained some weight, and looked more beautiful than before. Everything around him felt fresh and blooming. He gave a faint smile in response to Raani's comment and entered the temple.

'Dei, what is this? Why abandon your game and rise just because I've walked in? Resume your game...'

'Saamiyappo! Do you know what state you were in the past few days? As Raani said, you seemed to be in a trance. This artist grabbed the opportunity and kept on painting. You were seated as if you were tranquilized using chloroform... Eyes closed and breath steady... I came calling on you several times, but you gave no response! I heard from Parvathi that you were having the milk and food that she was preparing for you every day. That's when I was relieved that nothing was wrong with you. Raani was worried when she came there once and you didn't show any signs of recognition. I've known you from the time when Lakshmi Amma was around... When you're engrossed in reading, you forget even food and water...'

'Velappa, you're in Saami's way now... Move aside, let's open the doors. Let Saami proceed for his prayer.'

Vengu smiled at Guruswamy and stepped aside as if to say he didn't need to be instructed.

'Raani... Looks like your husband has settled for an idle game now instead of going to work? Has he grown bold that he has a son now, or does he not listen to you any more?' Guruswamy asked Raani.

'Saamiyappo... He works at the Dairy Society now, doesn't he? He has Tuesdays off every week. That's why he's gathered company for a game.'

'Dairy Society? How come? Aren't your brothers board members there? How could he have landed a job there?'

'No, it belongs to a different union. It's a cooperative society formed by labourers who have invested small amounts as shares. He has also taken five or six shares of ten rupees each. He came to tell you this news a few days ago, but you were in that state. Oh, you must see how he walks, reads papers and behaves these days... Like a leader... He also gives me lectures sometimes... Also, Saamiyappa, there's another important thing. I wasn't sure whether to tell you or not. He has started smoking cigarettes and beedis. And to add to that...'

'Ei, you're going too far. That's enough,' Velappan interrupted hotly, glaring at her.

Then, turning towards Guruswamy, he said, 'It's nothing, Saamiyappo… Don't mind her. She thinks even now that she lives in that wealthy farmhouse. I pawned her necklace to arrange for the money to buy shares for the dairy society. After buying the shares, we pooled some money together and had coffee. She has been grumbling since then.'

'Here, look into my eyes and say if it is coffee that I'm talking about.'

'Raani, let it go… Bring me that little boy… See how he smiles at me! Did anyone from your family come to see the child?'

'Saamiyappa, I don't have anyone to call my people there any more… Only you and these neighbours here are my kin now. When we were in Madurai, do you know to what lengths they went to with those henchmen at their service? If they really had any love for their sister, they wouldn't have dared to do any of that! Even if what I did was wrong, how could they go that far? Wait here, I'll change the baby's clothes and bring him.'

'Raaniyamma, what's wrong with his clothes now? I don't mind if he's wet himself. Give him here. Dei, my dear… Come here… Yes, like that… You little darling…'

Watching Guruswamy crooning with the baby in his arms, Velappan and the others laughed in surprise.

'What's there to laugh? Did you all think I couldn't handle a baby? If Subbu were alive, we would've somehow had a child, and I would've done this and even more, to him…'

Even though Guruswamy said it lightly, Raani noticed a hint of pain on his face.

'Saamiyappo, give him to me before he passes urine on your white clothes.'

Just as Raani was stretching her arms to collect the baby, he promptly urinated on Guruswamy's dhoti and the towel he wore on his shoulder.

'Now that's a true punishment. 'Where have you been the past six days? Have this!' is your way of exacting revenge for my absence, isn't it? Now go, go to your mother.' He handed the infant to Raani.

Turning towards Vengu and sitting on the temple pial, he asked, 'Yes, Bhagavathar… How are things in Chaalai circle?'

'I'll fetch a fresh set of clothes from the clothesline upstairs,' Velappan called as he ran upstairs.

2

PARVATHI HAD TIDIED UP GURUSWAMY'S ROOM AND MOVED on to washing the dishes in the kitchen when Velappan entered the house. There was also something boiling on the stove. Velappan pulled a dhoti that was hung on the clothesline and turned to leave when a smoky picture framed on the corner of the wall caught his attention. He looked at it carefully. It was a picture of a pretty woman, completely naked, with full breasts and firm thighs. What was this? He had been to this room hundreds of times before, and yet, his eyes had never fallen on this picture before. He had seen the other pictures – those of Swami Vivekananda, Buddha and Jesus Christ… Of all days, why did his eyes spot this dull picture – hidden in plain sight among many others – today? Hmm… When Velappan walked back, his pace had slackened considerably.

'Velappa, that pretentious monk who owns and resides in the grove you live in… He's also a bourgeois… They have had a tendency across generations. They pretend to be devout, profess to help poor people and act as if they have renounced everything. But deep inside, they are a deadly breed. You have been hoodwinked all these years, blindly believing him to be a divine soul. If he is indeed a true friend of the working class, ask him if he is ready to hand over his entire plantation to the labourers in the grove. People like him have deep-seated desires when it comes to matters of money and women. You will see the truth for yourself slowly. Keep reading. Read good books that put forth progressive ideas. That's how you become a serious proletariat. There is nothing progressive in buying a few shares and calling yourself a labourer.'

Several liberal ideas were discussed in the weekly meetings conducted by the Dairy Society. Were these words, spoken to him by a fellow labourer at one such meeting, gaining a new light today? That was when Velappan began rethinking his understanding of Guruswamy from the beginning.

He stood on the top of the stairs and watched Guruswamy, who was seated downstairs on the temple pial, listening to Vengu Bhagavathar's impassioned commentary on the Chaalai circle's present state.

'Saami, it doesn't matter if it's six days or sixty days… Even if it pours cats and dogs, Chaalai doesn't change much. You have told us how Diwan Kesavathaasan created this Chaalai Bazaar during the time of King Marthandavarman, haven't you? This market looks the same as it was then; nothing has changed. But the people who run it are not the same any more. It's changing drastically. Who you see today at the market cannot be found in two days' time… People keep drifting. Earlier, just after I had moved here from Ottankadai, when I sang a song standing at one of the intersections, my bag would be full with coins within half an hour. It's not so easy these days… I roam all across the place – from Aryasalai corner to the fort on the east, then through the Karikkadai corner, Kothuvaal Street, and the full length of Karuppattikkadai Road to see a decent collection.'

'Oh, things have changed so much, you say?'

'Yes… Faces in the market keep changing. Some days, when I walk along the street singing one of Pattinatthaar's devotional songs, some men whistle indecently while others ask for film songs. There are very few familiar faces in the bazaar… It is because of them that I can make a living… There is a Chettiyar in the bazaar – a pawnbroker… He's been there since—'

'Vei, Bhagavathar, stop there. He just asked how things were, and you keep on prattling about old times… Saami has come down after almost a week. Let him pray to Devi in peace,' Pappan interrupted abruptly.

'Let it be, Pappa. How's your work going?'

'Not bad, Saami. People use stainless steel utensils these days. As Bhagavathar said, things have indeed changed a lot. Who owns brass and copper vessels these days? What reason do people have to approach a tinker any more? Anyway, I live near the Devi temple. Thanks to her generosity, these are a few customers who still need my services. For the past few days, I've been repairing vessels from a tea shop on the Power House road.'

'You shut me up a minute ago, and now you're narrating your history. Here, Velappan has brought Saami's dhoti at last. Let's get back to our work.'

Velappan was observing Guruswamy intently as he descended the stairs. He saw the dark, black beard, the serene face and the pure heart that shone through Guruswamy's words.

Bourgeois! What an ugly word!

But what about that picture? Had it been there all these years, only to appear in front of his eyes today? Perhaps he had seen it before without registering it. Perhaps his mind had been straight then. Today, when his thoughts were polluted, the picture seemed to have appeared before him in a new light. Maybe this is what they call 'coloured by perception'. It was impossible to understand anyone these days.

'Velu, you ran up the stairs so energetically, and now you're coming down so lethargically... Bring the dhoti here. I'll take a walk to the end of the street. By the time I'm back, the temple will also be open. I'm going upstairs only after I've finished my prayer today,' Guruswamy said, changing into the new dhoti. He walked to the left and reached the rear of the temple and stood there thirstily watching the gigantic painting of Devi on the back wall. After a few moments of meditation, he walked down the narrow path bordered on both sides by a thick outgrowth of nettles and touch-me-nots.

'These need to be trimmed... Can't walk peacefully through this outgrowth...'

When Guruswamy reached the road, the shopkeeper at the laundry store stood up respectfully.

'It's rare to see you these days, Saami,' he said, to which Guruswamy responded with a smile and walked on.

Everyone stood watching him until he reached the end of the road and disappeared from sight.

'What a great man! Look at how humble and serene he is even in this day and age... You can't find men of his type any more.'

'Tough to say whom to believe and whom you can't these days,' Velappan muttered to himself as he threw away the half-smoked cigarette and entered his house. Raani, who was rocking the cradle when he came in, smiled at him and said, 'I've been rocking it for an hour now, but the little devil doesn't want to fall asleep. He's wide awake and hardly blinking, but quiet all the same. He has learnt all these mischievous ways from his father. Why are you so quiet? Oh, are you mad at me that I told on you to Saamiyappa?'

'Shut up, you idiot! Not knowing when and what to speak...'

'It's come this far, is it? I see you don't have the same love for me these days. We're wedded, and after all these days, we have a baby, too. That's all, isn't it? I've become an idiot now. Lately, this is the kind of language you're using on me. Who else do I have other than you? You can call me an idiot or a bitch, you can beat me up or even kill me... Who can question you any more?'

'Raani, what's this? Can't a man be at peace on a week off? I now regret going upstairs to fetch Saami's dhoti. Now, as soon as I'm home, you've started howling about something!'

'Look at me. What's gotten into you today? Tell me... What happened when you went to fetch his clothes?' Raani asked, closing the distance between them and lifting his chin in her palm.

She leaned on him and kissed him softly on his lips.

'Thoo, thoo... You stink of cigarettes... You won't listen to me if I ask you to stop this nasty habit, will you?'

She pinched his lips in mock anger.

'Did you just pinch me? I'll give you something in return...'

He hugged her tightly and bit her lips.

'Aah, it hurts... Let go of me... Either you behave like a saint, or you go to the other extreme. That's enough. There's time until nightfall. The baby is also awake...'

'As if he sleeps during the night. How does it matter? Come here...'

'The door is open, and I still have work to do in the kitchen.'

'Don't you resist when I pull you—'

Just as Velappan pulled her into a tight hug, Guruswamy's voice was heard from the outside.

'Velappa!'

'He just left for some place so purposefully. He's already back, your bogus monk,' Velappan muttered under his breath in disappointment and anger.

'Don't speak so rashly about Saamiyappa just because your desire has been doused. Give some respect.'

'Of course, your dear Saamiyappa!' he murmured as he rose, and then called out loudly, 'I'm coming.'

3

THE SUN WAS SLOWLY RISING. WHEN GURUSWAMY CAME OUT to the terrace and looked down, he saw Raani's child standing on its feet and playing with its hand inside a water pot. The smile that was concealed by his beard showed in his eyes. The child was growing up fast. It felt like only yesterday that Velappan came up the steps excitedly to inform him that Raani had given birth to a boy. He tried to shake off his thoughts and pull his mind into a meditative state. His eyes shrank against the bright sunlight. His eyes had lately become sensitive. Where was that bold man who could unflinchingly stare at the midday sun and construct the majestic image of the deity Akilandeshwari in his mind's eyes? *Chi, stop racing, you fickle mind... Stop...* In the light that flooded his eyes, Raani's child stood smiling, holding on to a pot. He looked like the child form of Lord Krishna, who stood with a mischievous smile, traces of stolen butter smeared all over his body. Raani came out of her house carrying a basket, carefully collecting hibiscus flowers from the plant in the yard and dropping them in the basket. She looked beautiful… She looked like an elegant flower herself… A flower with closely formed petals…

Vengu's voice drifted in from somewhere along with his percussion beats: 'The forehead that I worship, the shapely shoulders, and the lovely breasts…'

As the focus that Guruswamy was fighting to attain kept slipping out of his hand like a thrashing fish, desire splashed chaotically in his mind.

'Raani! Look at your Saamiyappa on the terrace. These days, his gaze has become that of a fox staring at a hen coop… His wife passed away at a young age… Now, what do you suppose he reads all day, sitting alone in his abode? Oh, I can't even begin to tell you… I, too, considered him like a father. Only now do I realize how foolish I've been!'

'Don't let your tongue wag. The company you keep nowadays has made you critical of everything. Saamiyappa has also become a victim of it. It is a sin to speak ill of him, mind you. You should not forget your place just because you earn better now. He has given us this home, he helped us get married… Had he not been there to support us when my brothers sent some men to finish us off…'

'Silly woman! Even educated women are nothing but idiots. Of course, birds of the same feather, aren't you two? I'm a Malayali... That fraudster Saami is a Tamilian, like you... Now, listen... Our association is constructing living quarters for all the employees. Once that's ready, we're vacating this filthy place immediately. My only worry is that this Saami doesn't grab hold of your hand before that day comes,' Velappan said, guffawing loudly.

'Don't laugh and make a fuss. Saamiyappa is praying to the sun.'

Velappan pinched Raani affectionately.

'Aiyo, so early in the morning!' she chided him and hurried into the house to drop the distasteful topic. Velappan lit up a cigarette and sent up a mouthful of smoke upwards, in the direction of Guruswamy. The child toddled towards Velappan eagerly.

'Dei, little devil... Your mother is inside the house. Go to her, go.'

When Guruswamy went into his house, the sun had risen fully.

Had everything changed completely? Devotion, faith, fear, respect, humility... They had all transformed into something else today. What once was a majestic kite had shrunk into a moth or a vermin that wallowed in the mud! A lowly life had now lifted its head to defy him!

Truth be told, he deserved to be slandered. This change was absolutely necessary.

Raani's son had started walking now. Velappan had become the association leader at the milk society. Alcohol and insubordination were part of him now. His respect towards Guruswamy had plummeted. What began as bitter words uttered to Raani within the confines of their home had now become open taunts. Everyone was surprised by his sudden disrespect towards Guruswamy. How could he have transformed into this?

'The nerve of him! He's the association leader now. After all, anyone who enters a business in Chaalai Bazaar is cursed to renounce his parents and his god, isn't he?'

'Velappa, you have grown in status and earned a respectful post. So be it… But never be ungrateful! You should remember you reside in Saami's land and in the vicinity of the Devi temple—'

'Quit your sermons! I know enough. No one needs to teach me manners.' Velappan cut the conversation short.

Everything around the plantation had changed. Pappan was now a salaried employee in a utensil store in Chaalai. His wife worked as a maid at a bank officer's house in Valiyasalai. His seven-year-old eldest son was in first grade at a Tamil school. The other two kids still played in the sand banks of the canal inside the plantation.

Vengu was now interested in Tamil literature, in addition to his street singing. These days, he went regularly to the Tamil library to read novels and stories. 'Tamil writers of today write explicitly all the sensual things that were handled subtly in old literature. That's okay... It helps pass the time and also satiates the desire,' he even philosophized once.

Artist Ravi was putting off earning jobs like painting hoardings and was fervently pursuing 'art'. He often recounted fondly how people from the Government Arts College had paid five hundred rupees to buy one of his paintings – it was a picture of an ample-bosomed Malayali woman clad only in a towel around her bust, pouring liquor out of a pitcher into the waiting mugs of customers in a bar. For some time, he went around claiming that his portrait of Guruswamy was his masterpiece. When he wanted to make an occasion out of the unveiling ceremony of the portrait – a congregation in the temple yard – Guruswamy had flatly refused to entertain it. Looking at the painting when it was eventually brought to his home, Guruswamy was amazed at how realistic it was. He realized how important a clear mind was for an artist, more than skill. How could Ravi, whose occupation was to paint for hoardings and write in cursive letters, paint a portrait of him? Guruswamy had consented to pose for the painting only to test Ravi's skills, but he was exhilarated when the painting was done. On the day the painting arrived at Guruswamy's house, he went inside the pooja room and came back with a few five-hundred-rupee notes and pushed them into Ravi's hands. The artist had burst out crying. That was the biggest reward he had received for his art in his entire life. Naturally, for the next few months, he sang praises of Guruswamy wherever he went. Then, showing Guruswamy's painting as proof of his art, he received some money in advance from a wealthy landlord in the Chaalai circle to paint his portrait. After almost a year, it was still in the making. The landlord's servant came to Ravi's house often to enquire about it and invariably yelled at him. It was during this time that the picture of the liquor lady earned him more fame. Nowadays, Ravi could be found cutting out pictures of naked women from English magazines and trying to copy them on canvas. He had started wearing shirts with floral patterns, grown his hair up to his collar, chewed betel leaves and often assumed a ruminative pose like 'artists' do.

In the plantation, which was witnessing such rapid transformations, Parvathi was the only creature who remained immutable. She had the same dry, disheveled hair and the same old, faded sarees. She still did the same chores – sweeping the temple yard and Guruswamy's house clean every day, picking every single hibiscus flower from the plants and making garlands out of them for Devi, watering Guruswamy's favourite garden space and washing his dishes. She didn't even seem to have aged.

'Since Raani Ammai makes spicy and tangy food nowadays, Saami has begun having two proper meals a day,' she sighed contentedly, as if that filled her heart more than anything else. Whenever Velappan heard her say this, he bit her head off: 'Let your saami marry a woman. She'll cook delicious food for him and take care of other things, too.'

'Have you gone mad? Why are you mouthing off like this?'

'You imbecile! Shut your mouth, or I'll shut it for you!'

'Oh, Devi! Can people change so much?' Parvathi turned towards the temple helplessly with folded hands and a disturbed heart.

4

AS THE CHILD SLOWLY PLACED HIS HANDS AND FEET DOWN and dragged himself up the steps, Raani came running anxiously to pick him up.

'Aiyo! Is Saamiyappa not at home? This boy is a nuisance,' she cried as she reached the bottom of the stairs.

Guruswamy, who was at the stove making something for his lunch, came out immediately. He saw Raaja, the little child, climb the steps faster than before to evade his mother, who was already coming up. Guruswamy bent and picked up the child.

'Looks like you'll grow up to be naughtier than your father,' he playfully chided the boy before turning to Raani and inviting her inside the house.

'Yes, I was going to visit you anyway, Saamiyappa,' she replied, climbing the last few steps and entering his home. She gaped at the full-length portrait of Guruswamy in the hall as if she were seeing it for the first time. Then, smiling to herself, she picked up a Tamil magazine from the table.

'Saamiyappa, do you read these magazines? Aiyo, Tamil magazines these days are not worth reading. The kinds of stories and the illustrations that come with them... I don't know if my husband saw any of these when he came up, but he has been bad-mouthing you a lot lately.'

'Leave it aside... He has the right to say anything about me. After all, you can speak freely only of people you take rights with. In other cases, you'll have to justify what you say. Anyway, the rice is boiling on the stove. Can you take care of it? Also, what did you want to visit me about? Did you have another fight with him? Raaja, did your mother and father fight again?'

Raaja giggled as if he had understood what Guruswamy asked. He slipped away from Guruswamy, ran to his mother and hid his face behind her saree. Raani picked him up and gave him back to Guruswamy before she went to the stove.

'It was about three in the morning when he came home from work... Hopelessly drunk... He has been drinking a lot nowadays. I got up, opened the door and went back to bed. He came straight at me as if he was going to kick me. I moved aside at the last moment. 'Why don't you finish me off instead? Who's going to question you? You'll also be rid of me for good,' I cried. 'He beat me up heavily after that, Saamiyappa. I can't handle this any more... Please have a word with him. Do I deserve this kind of life? I feel silly to have blindly followed my instincts and married him,' she sobbed.

'Raaniyamma, what is this? Since when did you start weeping like Parvathi or Pappan's wife? You are an educated woman. Even when you eloped with him, you told me you were well aware of what you were getting into. He's not an elite man of profound thought or action. You have to patiently change his ways. Moreover, as you mentioned only a while ago, he has no respect for me any more.'

'I have been observing this for some time, Saamiyappa. I'm at my wits' end. I didn't believe it when people told me these things might happen. Didn't you see how he abuses Parvathi? Weren't you a quiet witness, too? Yes, he doesn't respect you even a little. I didn't want to bring it up, but you are the only support I have here. The other day, when he said something, I threatened him that I would tell you. He simply said, "To hell with you and your bogus Saami!"'

'Raani, it is my fault that he speaks so of me now. Isn't it my fault that I let him be as he pleased from the time he came to me as a child? I should have let you two find your own way after you married and went off to Madurai.'

'If you had let us go like that, I would probably be dead by now. It is Devi's grace that I'm still alive, even if it's only amidst all the swearing and beating. You are the one consolation I have.'

'Be careful with it. Don't get carried away by our conversation and spill the hot stuff over yourself!'

'Don't you have some curry or gravy to have this with?'

'Since Parvathi became bedridden, I've had to make do with curd and tamarind or citron pickles. For some time, you used to bring whatever you made at home. After Subbu passed away, I had trained my tongue to survive on bland food. Then you came along and spoiled me with the taste of good food. But after Velappan changed for the worse, you don't come here frequently either...'

'Don't you worry. I'll come here as I please, no matter what he says. It's all because of this little devil. He doesn't let me finish any work. Even now, I had just sat to scrape some coconut and make a roasted paste. When you have to run behind him wherever he goes, nothing gets done. Anyway, I'll prepare the paste and bring it before you sit for lunch.'

'Listen, Raani... Don't bring any of these spicy, tasty

things to me any more. Let me be by myself. These people call me a monk if I keep to myself. Am I wearing saffron or what? Back to what we were discussing... Tell him I asked for him when he comes home, will you? I hope he's not yet lost his senses completely. It's the drink and the new company he keeps that's talking. Let Raaja be here. You go, take care of your work. Velappan will be back in the afternoon, won't he?'

As if on cue, Velappan's voice was heard from the temple yard: 'Ei, Raani... Mahaaraani! Where on earth have you gone?'

'Aiyo! He's here... I'll go, Saamiyappo!'

'Send him up right away if he's not drunk,' Guruswamy called after her descending figure.

When the child tried to wriggle out and follow his mother, Guruswamy held him tight and brought him into the house.

A few minutes later, he heard loud noises from below – unmistakable sounds of a quarrel. Deciding that it was not right to stay quiet any more, Guruswamy went down with the boy in hand.

'Why stealthily visit him in broad daylight? Why don't you go sleep with him at night, too? After all, it is the filthy blood of the rich that runs in you, too. That's probably why you readily ran away with me, a lowly milkman. Who knows what Konaar or Nair men you were in touch with before that! I know everything about all the so-called elite men in Chaalai circle.'

'Say whatever pleases you about me. Don't you dare speak ill of Saamiyappa, who is like a god to us. Devi won't forgive you for that...'

'Oh, you and your Devi... Where was your deity when that old Parvathi put her hand into boiling porridge? Look how she has been bedridden, moaning and whining. Can't your Devi come down and give her relief? Raani Amme, don't talk to me about your Devi or that bogus Saami... I'll slap you!'

When Velappan turned around, seething, he saw Guruswamy standing outside, in the temple yard, and fell quiet for a moment.

'Are you done? I was listening to everything. Are you leaving already? It would be nice if you could come up for a minute,' Guruswamy said, handing over the child to Raani and hurrying up the stairs without a backward glance.

5

HE WAITED A WHILE FOR VELAPPAN TO COME UP. Meanwhile, he rehearsed what he would say. Velappan, however, never showed up. What words he had uttered! Poor Raani, what did she know! How had Velappan seen into his heart to speak like that? Guruswamy smiled to himself. Was a storm brewing in the quiet life he had led so long? He deserved it. Every life needs its share of storms. How much longer could he go on living a bland life?

What had Velappan seen in him to fling words like that? Even as a child, when Velappan had followed him to the temple halls, he never seemed to have caught the drift of Guruswamy's mind. 'Saamiyappa, how long are you going to keep staring at these statues of women? Aren't we going to pray?' he had often asked innocently. He was still a naive man. Thinking back about how he had guided and supported Velappan at every turn of his life to make the sailing smooth, Guruswamy could not make sense of Velappan's recent transformation.

When he had learnt of Velappan's involvement in the processions, chants and labour strikes organized by the clueless labour unions of Chaalai Bazaar, Guruswamy had thought Velappan would learn his lesson as time passed. When he had found out about his drinking habit and how he abused Raani, he had told Velappan off a couple of times. Disregarding those early signs had resulted in its growth into a giant tree today. Velappan was hurling the thorny branches of the tree at the very same man who watered it. What happened a few days ago to Parvathi was a terrible thing, though. Guruswamy was helpless, unable to contront Velappan even after that incident. Poor Parvathi!

It was a Friday. When Guruswamy heard that Velappan was responsible for the special prayer at the Devi temple that day, he had felt relieved that all was not as bleak as it seemed. He had thought Velappan was not beyond redemption and that his devotion and loyalty had not disappeared altogether. Velappan had asked Pappan early that evening to prepare a generous quantity of paayasam with rice and jaggery.

'Pappa Anne! I'm bringing five to six members of the union for today's special prayer. Let the paayasam be delicious!'

Later in the evening, the priest came and lit all the

lamps. When a couple of boys from Paattu Vilaagam Street rang the temple bell loudly, Velappan appeared with his friends. 'Saamiye Saranam Aiyappa… Devi, Saranam Aiyappa… Saamiye Inquilab… Devi, Zindabad…' Their sarcastic calls could be heard even before they entered the temple premises. Parvathi finished tying up the garland and came straight to Guruswamy.

'Saami, there you are! Aren't you going to tell them off? It's your land, and it's our Devi they are making fun of. Aiyo, won't their tongues rot! And to think it is our own man who has brought such scoundrels, that, too, on a Friday… Come, please stop their atrocity,' Parvathi whimpered, close to tears.

Guruswamy gave his usual smile and said, 'Don't fret, Parvathi. They will make some noise and fall silent. Barking at the sun ruins only the dog's throat. Moreover, we can only tell Velappan off. I'd rather not do it in the presence of his friends. Let's see what more they have in stock. Now, give that garland to the priest… I'll be there in a minute.'

When Guruswamy came downstairs from his house, everything seemed normal. Velappan had completely stopped visiting or consulting Guruswamy for advice. Even on those few occasions when they crossed paths, he either slipped away quietly or hid himself so that there was no confrontation. He had even been paying – through Raani – a paltry amount as rent for the past few months. Guruswamy received it quietly to see how far these new changes had taken root. After the recent coconut harvest, when Parvathi took Velappan's usual portion of coconuts and firewood to him, he had refused it, saying, 'Parvathi, you can keep my share, too. I've bought enough firewood for my household already.'

'Landowners give you such things for free, and in turn, condition you to have a slavish attitude towards them. We naturally become their henchmen then. Let's forget how we've lived all these years. I'd like to avoid this beggarly lifestyle at least going forward.' He had also given a sermon in the presence of Pappan, Vengu and Ravi.

'I'm really pleased if he has become so self-reliant,' Guruswamy had responded when he heard of the incident.

However, Guruswamy remained a safe haven for Raani when she was distressed and Raaja's favourite uncle. This constantly piqued Velappan, sowing wild fancies in his inebriated mind.

As was his custom every Friday, Guruswamy finished his prayers at the temple, collected the prasadham in a leaf from the priest and returned to his house.

'Why didn't you give paayasam to Saamiyappa?' asked Raani, earning a hostile glare from Velappan.

After a few minutes, Parvathi, who was deep in prayer, went into a trance as usual. She stood there, shaking from head to foot, crying out unintelligibly. She looked like a woman possessed. The priest approached Parvathi and sprinkled kumkum on her face. Velappan and his friends began cackling, calling out, 'Devi, Saranam Aiyappa… Saamiye inquilab… Devi zindabad…'

'Velappa, you are treading perilously close to the fire in all your amusement. This isn't good for you.' The priest warned him and moved aside. Pappan and Vengu Bhagavathar stood in a corner, uneasy and anxious. A small group of women and children was gathered around the hot pot of paayasam.

Velappan came forward excitedly and snatched the ladle from Pappan's hand, saying, 'Give it here, Pappan Anne! Let's present the first serving of the paayasam to Devi and get her blessings.'

He scooped up a ladleful of piping hot paayasam and poured it in the outstretched hands of Parvathi, who was still in her trance.

The next moment, Parvathi wailed aloud, shaking her hands vigorously, and fell unconscious. Even then,

Velappan and his companions kept chanting, 'Saamiye inquilab… Devi zindabad…' amidst derisive laughter.

It was Vengu Bhagavathar who immediately came to Parvathi's aid. He lifted her with the help of a couple of women and took her away.

'Bhagavathar! Nothing will happen to Parvathi. It was, after all, in Devi's hands that I poured the paayasam. It is Devi who has descended on her, you see. She'll protect Parvathi from any kind of heat. She's a powerful deity!' Velappan guffawed, with his friends joining in the chorus.

Raani was mortified at what had transpired. She picked up her sleeping child and went into the house, shutting the door loudly behind her. Pappan's wife and a few other women carried her to her hut to give her first aid.

Displeased with the ruckus downstairs and the episode involving Parvathi, Guruswamy shut himself inside his pooja room. He knew how badly Parvathi was hurt only the next morning: Both her palms looked puffed and inflamed. When Pappan and Vengu took her to the hospital for treatment, Guruswamy accompanied them. His made-up account of a hot water accident was accepted without question at the hospital.

How had Velappan turned so vile all of a sudden? How had he acquired such bitter hatred that he spoke and acted so contemptuously even while he resided on Guruswamy's land? Guruswamy was overwhelmed with surprise and agony the more he thought about it.

6

RAANI TOOK CHARGE OF SOME OF PARVATHI'S ROUTINE TASKS in her absence. Meanwhile, Raani's frequent visits to Guruswamy's house incited wild visions in Velappan's mind, which, of late, had led to obscene taunts about Raani and Guruswamy. The more he provoked her, the more she went to Guruswamy. Meanwhile, she was also taking care of feeding and assisting Parvathi, who was weak and bedridden.

'Aiyo, I wonder how Saami Aiya managed without hot water for his shower! Oh, Devi… Isn't today Tuesday? The temple yard needs to be washed and cleaned… Saami would also love some stew made with drumstick leaves… Why has Devi left me in this state! I don't blame anyone… I must've done something wrong for Devi to punish me through their act of mischief… Devi, please forgive this poor woman…' Parvathi whined all day.

'Be calm, Parvathi. You committed no sin. Devi will definitely make those sinners pay. There's nothing wrong with you now. I'm here to take care of Saamiyappa. I care about him just as much as you do,' Raani consoled her.

'I know the responsibilities you have taken up, and I also hear all the things your husband calls you for it. You came here with him, leaving behind your people and the home you grew up in! Do you deserve this beggarly life under a thatched roof? Aren't you a queen, my dear? What a palatial house and regal family you had!' Parvathi wept.

Saddened by what she said, Raani quietly wiped her tears and returned to her house.

Why was he still a silent witness even after he had seen, heard and learnt everything there was to know? He wanted to summon Velappan in front of the Devi temple and confront him openly: 'What has gotten into you? How could you forget everything you learnt from here? You followed the footsteps of a milkman, became one yourself, fell in love with that innocent girl, and how dare you insult her now? Had I handed you over to those henchmen who gathered here to finish you off after your wedding, we wouldn't have had to witness all this commotion today! You do not know me fully yet, Velappa. Those men you now call your comrades will still listen to my words. You do not know even half of what I know about Chaalai Bazaar. Do you think you know better than I do? How dare you torture that poor girl, linking her with me! Get lost, you ungrateful swine. If I see you around my plantation again, I won't hesitate to resort to violence!' Guruswamy visualized these scenes over and over in his mind.

If he chased Velappan away from his land, what would Raani's plight be then? Raani… Raani… Raani could keep living comfortably in the security of the Devi temple and this neighbourhood. He was there to support her, too!

'Saamiyappa, I'm patiently enduring all this only in the solace that your presence gives me.'

'Yes, Raani, I'm here for you. I'm here. I'll always be.'

The white-necked kite soared in narrowing circles in the bright blue sky. The white of its head stood out in the daylight. Devi's majestic form grew bigger and bigger in his mind's eye and became one with the sculptures on the pillars of the Padmanaba Swamy Temple.

When his raging thoughts subsided at last, Guruswamy's eyes were wet with tears.

'Let it all come to an end on its own. No matter how high one soars, they need to touch ground in the end. Let us sit back and watch how far this goes…'

7

THE SUN WAS BLAZING DOWN. GURUSWAMY FELT THE HEAT of the day as he sat reading in his room. Was the heat a result of what he was reading, or was it emanating from his heart? He was sweating profusely even when he was idle. The ceiling fan, spinning at full speed, seemed only to be sending down hot air.

'Mangoooes, Mangoooes…' an old lady, who was selling mangoes from a basket, cried loudly. Raani had mentioned that two of Pappan's children were down with measles. The summer invariably brought these diseases. The Municipal Corporation had only recently proudly announced that smallpox had been completely eradicated. And yet, there was no remedy for measles. The corporation had sent a couple of nurses directly to Raani's home to vaccinate her child. Even Guruswamy and Raani were vaccinated. The crowd that thronged the Devi temple on Thursdays and Fridays had increased recently: People from the neighbourhood appeared sincerely twice a week to make food offerings and pray to the deity. Vengu had mentioned that measles was spreading rapidly in the surroundings of Chaalai, Paattu Vilaagam and Kamuku Vilaagam.

Guruswamy found it difficult to stay indoors any more. He stepped out onto the terrace. The air was still. The coconut trees hardly swayed. The copper roofing of the Aryasalai Temple glinted brightly in the sunlight. Even the crows were gathered in the shade of the banyan tree near the temple, hopping lightly and preening.

The brahminy kite was on the top branch of the usual tree, even in the midday heat. Could it feel the heat, too? A Malayali poet famously said a fan doesn't need the breeze. Dragonflies could be seen hovering over the bund of the temple's tank. The summer was, after all, a golden season for them. The brahminy kite did not seem to be bothered by the heat or afflicted with measles. They were Nature's children! Whose child was Man then? Diseases, drought, famine, heat, deluge, war, betrayal, desire, avarice – all these seemed to be reserved only for mankind!

There were loud noises coming from the direction of the road. In addition to calls of 'Catch him,' 'Beat him up,' and 'Kill him,' the sound of stones being pelted could also be heard. They were approaching the plantation.

The laundry shop and the betel leaves shop were boarded up hurriedly. Was that the sound of bottles breaking? Yes, bottles were also being hurled. A few shards of broken bottles fell in the temple yard. Two groups, wearing clothes of different parties, were involved in a tussle. Both parties dragged sacks of bottles – brought readily with them – onto the road and hurled them one by one at each other. The houses on the south end of the street were already shut. A dog caught in the sudden tussle ran away, howling in pain, bleeding from a fresh wound caused by glass shards. Loud obscenities… Taunts like 'Bring your leader here, we'll chop him up and feed him to the dogs…'

When Guruswamy came downstairs, the doors of Raani's and Pappan's houses were closed.

'Raani, the baby is with you, right? Stay inside. Shut the door tight,' he called out loudly.

'Saamiyappo! Don't go to the road. Go upstairs… Aiyo! Why did you come down now?' Raani shouted from inside the house.

'Saami… Go back to your room. There are murderous men on the streets. Devi! Saami Aiya won't even listen to me!' Parvathi cried from inside her house.

Pappan's two sons were watching the street through the small window of their house.

'Shut the window and stay inside. Is your father at home?'

'No, he's gone to work,' they responded in chorus before shutting the window.

A broken brick flew in from somewhere and landed on Guruswamy's shoulder.

'Go inside, you son of a dog!' someone yelled at him.

Before Guruswamy had time to figure out where the stone came from, his eyes dimmed, and he sat on the Devi temple's steps.

The laundry shopkeeper and a couple of boys who usually peddled on the streets came running from the roadside.

'Saami, you know better than to venture out now! Don't you know these barbarians don't care even about their fathers and mothers when they are in this state? Why did you come down now? We ourselves were hiding inside our shops. Aiyo, you're badly hurt! Oh, looks like something is broken. Bring that towel here! Yes, tie it up like that. He has to be taken to the hospital. Let's take Kamuku Vilaagam Street… If we find a taxi…'

'I'll bring a taxi. Let those beasts fighting on the road rot in hell,' one of the peddler boys volunteered and ran southwards.

Meanwhile, when police sirens were heard, everything

went silent, as if an invisible switch had been flicked off. Everyone ran away, making sure to obstruct the road with tins, bottles and sacks before they slipped away. When they had all left, the road looked in a bad shape – like freshly tilled soil.

All was quiet when the police force emerged from their van. They rounded up men from different corners and crammed them into their van. They also made enquiries at the neighbouring houses. The sun was hot and the roads were deserted by then, save for the cops and broken objects. A few dogs from the backyards of houses barked incessantly, realizing something strange had transpired in their neighbourhood.

When the taxi arrived, the policemen helped Guruswamy in and sent him to the hospital. Although he wasn't seriously injured, there was swelling where the stone had landed on his shoulder. The doctor wrapped a tight rubber bandage around the injured shoulder and sent him home.

Raani, Ravi, Pappan and Vengu were waiting to receive him, and they helped him up the stairs and onto his bed.

'Why did you come downstairs, Saamiyappo? I was shouting from inside the house, and yet, he was headed for the road.'

'Is Velappan back home, Raaniyamma?' Guruswamy asked. No one responded.

'Did he come home? Why do you stare blankly like that?'

'He's gone into hiding, evading arrest,' Vengu whispered hesitantly.

'The riot was caused by his party, wasn't it? The dairy society he works in, along with the labourers union of Chaalai Bazaar, have been competing with the members of the lorry drivers' association. One of Velappan's colleagues had stabbed a lorry driver at Vallakkadai the other day. What we witnessed in broad daylight was a retaliation for that. For almost an hour, they occupied our road and turned it into a battlefield. The policemen came only at the end. Thankfully, I found shelter at Naidu's bicycle shop on Angalamman Street. I saw Velappan drag a sack of bottles to the middle of the road and hurl one bottle after another at the other party. Saami, Raaniyamma… Don't mistake me. But how he has changed with the company he keeps these days… I have never witnessed something like this in our neighbourhood, Saami. He'll learn his lesson at last if he's caught by the police.'

Raani burst into tears at Vengu's last utterance. When Parvathi hurried to her side and tried to take the child from her, the boy began to bawl, too.

Guruswamy was also moved to tears.

'Saami, please calm down. Raaniyamma! What has happened now? The ruling party is in their favour. Even if the cops arrest Velu, they won't lay a finger on him. Moreover, his union president is a Member of Parliament. I heard he went to the police station immediately following the incident. If you're part of a union, a cooperative society or a political party and rise to the position of Secretary, these things are inevitable. There is always retaliation... Only someone ready for all that can enter those spaces. Still, he deserves this after all that he has done.'

'Vei, Bhagavathar! Stop there. Saami is already in a lot of pain. Don't you know when the right time is to show off your knowledge of these things? Let him rest for some time. Raaniyamma, don't worry about anything. Velappan is a smart fellow. He was smart enough to become the Secretary of the Dairy Society with just his fifth-grade education. Such small hiccups are to be expected in the life of someone who aims for greater things. He'll come back home safe, don't worry... Make some coffee or porridge for Saami. Come, let's all go downstairs. Come, boy... I'll buy you candies.' Pappan picked up the child and went down, followed by Parvathi and Vengu. Ravi was quiet throughout, as if he had lost something valuable. A few people – including a couple of women from the neighbourhood and a few shopkeepers – were waiting at the temple yard.

'Saami is fine… You can all go home… Ada, vacate the place, I say.' Pappan chased them away impatiently.

'Let them stay back and see Saami if they wish to. Why do you yell at them?' Ravi asked him in a low voice. He looked sombre as he returned to the pial of his house, where his painting supplies were strewn.

8

RAANI SAT BESIDE GURUSWAMY'S BED, SILENTLY WEEPING for several minutes. After everyone had left, Guruswamy closed his eyes and rested. Although the pain on his shoulder had subsided considerably, he realized there was a gaping wound in his heart.

Guruswamy remembered descending the stairs during the riot to check on Raani. He also remembered Raani warning him to go back to his room. When he returned to the foot of the stairs, he saw Velappan running down the road towards the house. But when Guruswamy turned around to get a better look, Velappan was nowhere to be found. Worried about where Velappan could have gone amidst all the chaos, Guruswamy headed towards the road. Suddenly, the brick came flying at him out of nowhere. He was sure Velappan would not have attacked him slyly like that. He was also sure that he had done no wrong to Velappan to deserve being pelted with a brick. Velappan was not so stone-hearted either. Perhaps it was a coincidence that Guruswamy was hit by a stone soon after he saw Velappan on the road. Why had the policemen asked him repeatedly if he knew who threw the brick at him? How could he have seen the assailant in all that commotion?

After struggling with such disturbing thoughts for a while, Guruswamy opened his eyes and found Raani still weeping by his bedside.

'Raani…'

She didn't seem to hear him.

'Raani, are you asleep?' he asked, trying to prop himself up on the bed.

'Ammov!' he cried, as a sharp pain shot up his shoulder.

'What is it, Saamiyappo? Why did you get up? Lie down… Rest a little.' Raani fussed over him, gripping him softly by his arms and lowering him on the bed.

Despite the pain, Guruswamy found something comforting in Raani's touch. He was experiencing a woman's loving, caring touch after several years.

'What else could I do? You were so lost in your own misery that you didn't even hear me call you.'

'Aiyo, did you really? I was lost in thought, Saamiyappo. What do you need?'

'Can you give me something to drink? I'm not sure if Parvathi has collected this evening's milk.'

'Yes, there's milk. I'll boil it and bring it now,' Raani said and headed to the kitchen. She lit the stove, mounted the milk vessel on it and returned to find Guruswamy staring at her.

'What is it, Saamiyappo?'

'Raani, I feel sad for you...'

'At least you are there to think of me, Saamiyappo! Who else do I have now? I never even dreamt that the man I trusted and eloped with would become this! I have a child now... If not for him, I could easily make a decision. We're all destined to die someday. I could have chosen to die sooner. But now, what would that child do without me?'

'Raani!' Guruswamy interrupted sharply. 'Let the others around here forget I exist. How could you forget that I'm here for you?'

'Saamiyappo! I may even forget god, but I'll never forget you. You are the only reason I feel peace even in this state. It is only after you that I think about my child.'

'Then what was that talk about staying alive only for the sake of the child?'

'I spoke without thinking, Saamiyappa.'

'Don't ever say anything like that again, Raaniyamma. Come, turn towards me now.'

Her eyes were still brimming with tears when she turned and looked at him.

'Come here... Let the milk be on the stove. Come closer...'

She stood beside his bed.

'Sit here.' Guruswamy pointed at the bed. The moment she sat on the corner of his bed, she broke into loud tears. Stroking her hair consolingly, Guruswamy took her hand and placed it on his chest.

'Don't cry, Raani,' he muttered softly and closed his eyes.

He felt no pain now. The gaping wound in his heart was healed. His mind felt clear like a cloudless sky. He could smell the fragrance of freshly bloomed flowers. All the lamps at the Devi temple were lit, gracing it with radiant beauty. Emerald snakes were slithering down the chains that held the lamps from the ceiling. A majestic painting of Devi smiled from the wall of the temple – with full breasts, an open vagina that contained within it all celestial spirits, numerous arms that branched from her torso, sharp teeth and a protruding tongue. Nectar flowed from the bowl she carried in one hand... Ammu Ammai, with her cat eyes and sweet voice, relieved herself from her father's embrace and approached him stark naked... She sang, 'Aambaadi thannil ore unniyundangane...' When he cried out to her not to leave him, Subbulakshmi sat there, fresh after a miscarriage, asking him demurely, 'Oh, do you know all the nuances of the art of sensuality?' Heavenly spirits flew around him, flapping their cloudy wings, singing, 'Intoxicated by love, I forget everything…' A solitary brahminy kite soared high above all these images. It left its usual tree in the distance and glided to the top of a red coconut tree in his grove. The majestic image of Devi was obscured by the dark shadow of the kite.

Feeling breathless, Guruswamy woke up. Raani stood beside his bed, holding a tumbler of hot milk in her hands.

'The milk had boiled, Saamiyappo. I didn't want to let it boil over. So, I gently got up without disturbing you… Here, be careful; it's hot.'

When Guruswamy collected the tumbler from her, he also took her hand in his.

'What is it, Saamiyappo?'

'Nothing… I'll have the milk. You better go down… It's very late. See if Velappan has returned. Raaja may also be asleep; go check on him,' he said, still holding on to her hand, and then releasing it hesitantly.

9

ON THE FIRST NIGHT OF MAY, THE SKY RAPIDLY BECAME overcast, and a heavy thunderstorm followed. The summer rain was a breath of fresh air to the dry land.

Guruswamy's shoulder was completely healed. Since summer started, he had begun to take a long walk for an hour as soon as he woke up every morning. These days, he was not interested in visiting temple halls and staring at sculptures on pillars. The most he did was visit the Devi temple and watch the paintings on its outer wall.

After the riot and the injury to his shoulder, he had not ventured out for two full weeks. Just when he had decided to resume his morning walks the next day onwards, the night rain poured promptly, as if to spoil his plans. He woke up only after six in the morning. When he came out to the terrace, he saw the effects of the rain on the street. The banner that Ravi had half painted and propped up on his pial was drenched in the rain, and the letters had been washed into streaks of colours. Guruswamy assumed that Ravi must still be asleep. Although the hibiscus plant in the temple yard had no leaves now, a few red flowers hung loosely after the rain like pieces of wet cloth. There were no coconuts on the trees either. A few flowers peeped from inside the yellow stalks of the fronds, like swords protruding through their sheaths. The cement pial of the temple had started drying up in patches. One corner of the cement floor was dry for a six-foot section – where someone had slept overnight despite the rain. Dark clouds remained on the horizon, allowing morning light to filter through slowly. The heat of the past few weeks had subsided, and a cool breeze drifted in.

Parvathi came up the stairs unsteadily, broom in hand, her saree draped over her shoulder like a blanket. Moving aside to let her in, Guruswamy went to the western end of the terrace. In the backyard of Raani's house, Velappan was brushing his teeth with charcoal. The black charcoal froth that dribbled from his mouth, and the way he cleared his throat and spat out saliva, got on Guruswamy's nerves. When Raaja came to play with the tub of water that Velappan had ready for brushing his teeth, he chided the child. 'Will you stay quiet for some time, makka? Ei, Maharaani! Take this boy inside. A man can't even brush his teeth in peace. Go, dear. Let father brush.' His tone mellowed gradually. *His face and that smile... Chi... Could he also be this gentle with the child? What a lousy fellow. He becomes a beast when he's drunk. What had that innocent girl seen in him to fall in love with him? Her youth and the monotony of a wealthy household had perhaps pushed her into this adventure!* When Guruswamy thought of her these days, a mellifluous tune seemed to fill his heart. The music he had left behind in time – why was it returning to him now? Poor girl... 'Saamiyappo, I may even forget god, but I'll never forget you...' Her eyes brimming with tears... 'Don't cry, Raani...' The softness of her hair under his fingers... What was that music that was rising from the depths of his heart? 'Intoxicated by love, I forget everything...'

What wicked thoughts! Guruswamy turned around, trying to clear his head, and saw Raani coming up to the terrace with milk bottles in hand.

'Raani, how come you're bringing the milk? Has Velappan left already? He hates to see you here.'

'He seems to be in a good mood today. He was playing with the child. Parvathi asked me to take the milk bottles up. Shall I boil the milk, Saamiyappo?'

'No, I'll take care of it, Raani. He's at home. You never know when his mood might change. Parvathi comes regularly these days, doesn't she? She was here this morning to clean the rooms. Let me boil the milk like I used to earlier. We all need to go back to our routine, don't we?'

'Oh, that's enough. You're still unwell. Let your body gain some strength first. I don't care who says what until then. He'll leave in a few minutes now. I'll come back and take care of everything,' she said, and went spiritedly down the stairs.

Subbulakshmi had never had this agility or liveliness. That was probably why she disappeared from his life, leaving behind memories that ached dully. 'What can we do against a force that's beyond our control?' he had consoled himself and lived all these years. Yet, like embers hidden in ashes, a spark still seemed to be alive in him, smouldering mildly.

Recently, when he had gone on one of his morning walks, he witnessed something at the bazaar. The street lights were still on during those hazy morning hours. On the porch of every shuttered shop, there lay people covered in blankets from head to toe, snoring loudly. There were derelict children, beggars, lepers and baggage bearers. Absorbed in how lousy life was for many people, he turned a corner and spotted four or five men sitting on the porch of a shop, smoking cigarettes. When he looked closer to see if he could recognize any face in the light thrown by the street lamp, he saw a man and a woman, stark naked, lying behind those men. It was only for a moment that he had witnessed it. 'Sir, it's nothing. Don't look this way. Just go on,' one of the men had said. He had spoken so nonchalantly, as if to say they were minding their business and asking him to mind his own.

Guruswamy had felt an odd disturbance in him throughout the day. He wished he had seen who that woman was. The light had been bright enough, and yet... How boldly she had been at that intersection in the middle of the market, taking advantage of the silence of the wee hours! These were progressive times indeed. Guruswamy was surprised that he did not feel the urge to wash himself clean after what he had witnessed. Instead, his mind kept replaying what he had seen, trying to see it better under brighter light.

The image he saw in the mirror had not changed a bit. Even at fifty, his beard was a dark black, without a hint of grey in it. Clear eyes, stiff lips and a bare, hairy chest... Notwithstanding the injured shoulder, he looked as majestic as always.

'Saamiyappa, what's with this new habit of looking at yourself in the mirror? Aiyo! The morning's milk I brought is there as I kept it! Haven't you had anything yet? Is this how you look after yourself? And you asked me not to bother when I offered to boil it!'

'I'm not hungry, Raani. Thoughts have been flowing one after another, and I got absorbed in them.'

'What are you thinking, looking in the mirror?'

'I was wondering why I should go around looking like a bear, with this thick beard and moustache. Why should I not shave everything off and be like a normal person?'

'So true, Saamiyappa! If you do that, you'll look like a thirty-year-old. You can even marry again. Honestly, I don't like this moustache and beard... They ruin your face!'

Humming a song under her breath, she headed to the kitchen and turned on the stove.

'Where do you keep the semolina? I'll make some porridge with it.'

'Raani, I hear excitement in your voice. Has Velappan promised to buy gold jewellery for you?'

'Who needs all that? It's enough if he speaks a few sweet words like he did today.'

'Oh, that's good news! He must be in a good mood today, then. Is he downstairs, or has he left?'

'He's gone out, taking the child with him. He went to the tailor to get a shirt and a pair of trousers stitched for Raaja. He also said something else. He has been elected as the vice president of the Dairy Society. So, we will also be given accommodation in the housing unit that belongs to the society. He was gushing about shifting residence right away this month.'

'Ada, our Velappan has become the vice president of the Dairy Cooperative Society! That's great news! Smart fellow indeed. If only he quits drinking and acts more prudently, he'll make a gem of a man.'

'I told him that, too. He swore on me and my child that he'll quit drinking. We were discussing this all night yesterday during the rain. It felt like forever since we spoke and laughed like that.'

'Oh, it is last night's memories that are flowing in the form of a song today,' Guruswamy commented playfully, carefully burying his face in the newspaper.

'You're a naughty man, Saamiyappa! Never trust a bearded man who looks like a saint! What was that knowing smile you gave when I said we discussed it all night yesterday?'

'It is precisely not to fool anyone with my appearance that I'm planning to shave off my beard…'

'I mean it, Saamiyappa. If you really take your beard off, you will be so handsome that I'll have to do some special ritual to ward evil eyes off you.'

'Raaniyammov, watch what you say. If Velappan comes back at this moment, he will fly into a rage hearing what you say.'

'Raani!' Velappan's loving call drifted up from the temple yard.

'Ada, your husband is capable of calling you so softly?'

'Yes, I'm coming.' Raani rushed down gleefully, even before Guruswamy had finished uttering his surprise.

Was his maths turning upside down? Were his calculations going awry?

How did it matter any more? Raani was going to leave soon. Guruswamy let out a deep sigh.

10

GURUSWAMY CHECKED HIS NEW LOOK IN THE MIRROR AND then raised his eyes to the portrait hung on the living room wall. The differences were so subtle. The man who stood before the mirror was not the man in the painting. The beard and the sharp gaze were the telling features of the portrait. The eyes that looked back from the mirror were stealthy eyes that brushed something under the carpet of his eyelids. Those stiff lips, broad forehead and long nose… He smiled as he thought of those lines: 'Saamiyappa, if you really take your beard off, you will be so handsome!' His heart swelled with pride. *Raani! If only you had said this before. Why don't you come see me now?*

When Guruswamy came out to the terrace, he noticed how much things had changed. The red coconut trees had freshly bloomed coconuts on them. The sun rising behind the Devi temple had a golden shine to it. Even Pappan, Parvathi, Vengu and Ravi looked new to him. The sky was new, and the earth was new as well.

Those men playing cards in the temple yard looked new to him, too.

'Things have taken a different turn now. You need to be smart to survive. All the employees of the utensils shop I work in have joined the union. Why should I be the only one to stand apart?' Pappan said, without taking his eyes off his cards.

'Of course... One has to change with changing times. Earlier, even if we started work at seven in the morning, we were allowed to have lunch by three or four in the afternoon. Even then, we were required to be back to work as soon as we were done eating. To think of the curses I've heard from the proprietor for being a few minutes late... And work used to go on until past midnight! There was no time to even take a leak. Thanks to all the dust and dirt we had to put up with in the grocery store, we ended up with asthma and TB. I doubt if there is one shop owner in Chaalai Bazaar without complaints of diabetes or piles. But things are changing gradually. The sons of those old shop owners have completed their college education and entered their fathers' businesses. The way things are run has also changed accordingly. We also have the Shop Act and Labourers' Laws now. We get one day off compulsorily every week.'

'Yes, don't we, too, deserve to waste our time playing cards like this?' Ravi laughed.

'Oh, what care do you have? You have your paint and some fools to give you business. Every day in the week is a day off for you. You earn a lot to paint half-naked pictures of foreign women. Do you still paint pictures of deities and saints these days? At best, you paint banners with the slogan "Victory to the revolution!"'

'Dei, you need some brains for that. The art of painting is not a mundane task like mending vessels. Venkatachala Bhagavathar... Why are you so quiet?'

'What do I have to say? What do I know, apart from watching you play and listening to you talk? I can sing a song, if you like...'

'Vei, vei, Bhagavathar... Don't start one of your sour songs. I don't want to rush to the toilet right now.'

As the group broke into laughter, Velappan emerged from his house carrying his child. Guruswamy, who had until then stood listening to the conversation and laughter from his terrace, went back into his house immediately. He did not want Velappan to see his transformation.

'What's with the loud chatting and laughter?' Velappan asked lightly. The men gathered to play cards shifted as if to stand up in respect.

'Sit down, sit down. Keep playing. This boy doesn't let me be at peace if I'm at home. He wants me to carry him around all the time. I'm taking him for a walk until the end of the road,' Velappan said, leaving them to their game.

'How come Pappan and Bhagavathar said nothing to him? Are you scared of Velappan now?' Ravi prodded them.

'Why would we be? He, too, used to pick coconuts in this plantation with us, didn't he? He doesn't even respect our saami these days. Whether he becomes the vice president of the Dairy Society or the chief minister of this state, he will always be the same Velappan to us.'

'Oh, we'll see... You will keep treating him this way only if he stays here forever. He will soon be moving out of this plantation, you'll see...'

'That's the last thing he'll do! Do you know what his plan is? All of us have been living on this land for generations now. Saami doesn't have an heir either. So, Velappan calculates that we can all legally claim the portions we live in for ourselves. He now has political backing as well. All things said and done, he's a Malayali, isn't he? He should be credited for his smartness.'

'Don't go on prattling. Saami was there on his terrace until a few minutes ago. He went inside only now. Did you see him? He, too, has changed a lot. He has shaved off his beard and moustache and looks like a totally different man. Did you notice that the other day, after the coconut harvest, he asked Raani to take about fifty extra coconuts? He doesn't care much for Parvathi nowadays. She's grown old and falls sick frequently. I think we'll see a funeral soon.'

'Voi, foolish tinsmith. Your thinking has definitely seen a turn ever since you became a salaried employee in that shop. I blame it all on the unions, political parties and the dailies.'

'Painter sir… Why don't you try painting a portrait of Saami with his new look? We'll know the depth of your art then. Do you think you can?'

'Do you think I can't?'

'Vei, painting a beard is simple. Two strokes of paint do the trick. But you'll have to pay more attention to the entire face and capture every detail of it. A wrong stroke, and the whole face will be ruined on canvas. Why don't you give it a try now?'

'Get up now, Bhagavathar. Look there, Saami is coming down. Go, sing a couple of your devotional songs. He'll give you a nice slap with his slippers.'

Laughing gaily, they all rose to their feet.

11

IT WAS THE USUAL STRIKE THAT WAS STAGED EVERY ONAM season. As Onam day grew closer, the relationship between the workers' unions and business owners grew more and more unstable. Since both the labourers' union of Chaalai Bazaar and the Dairy Cooperative Society in which Velappan worked belonged to the same parent union, it gained incredible strength and organized rallies at all times of the day, which went around chanting slogans and cursing the business owners. The demand from the labourers was a 50 per cent higher hike in the annual bonus compared to the previous year. When the labourers' union was stubborn in its demand, leaving no room for compromise, the Chamber of Commerce – the union comprising business owners – responded with an equally stubborn no-hike-in-bonus policy. Representatives from the labourers' union, the Chamber of Commerce and authorities of Industrial Management met in the presence of the district collector to arrive at a mutually agreeable solution. The business owners argued that they had no choice but to close their businesses during the festival season every year, thanks to the unreasonable demands put forward by the labour unions. The representatives of the labourers threatened to bring the protests to the doors of the bourgeois owners' houses if they closed their businesses.

When both sides were obstinate in the expression of their respective stances, business owners decided to show their displeasure by closing their stores, and most shops in Chaalai Bazaar greeted the festive days of Onam with shuttered doors.

By this time, the labourers' movement had become more serious. When the employees of the Dairy Cooperative Society orchestrated a one-day strike condemning this move of the business owners, milk supply to the entire town got cut, seriously affecting many people. More than the impact it had on tea shops and domestic households, its repercussions in hospitals and orphanages made people realize the strength of the protest. The rhetoric of 'Would it hurt the profit-seeking owners to give a small hike in the annual bonus of poor, struggling labourers?' gained popularity among the people. When the protestors gathered outside the houses of the business owners learnt that they had popular support as well, their approach changed. When they chanted obscenities about the women of those households, and when it also became physical at times, the police had to intervene, despite their policy of non-interference in business affairs. The clash between the labourers and cops intensified into a riot. The first police force that arrived in a van was welcomed with stones pelted by the labourers from every nook and corner. The armed policemen could not be expected to surrender without a fight, could they? They resorted to a blind, violent attack against the assailants with their batons. Velappan was at the head of one of the protesting factions that day. He also happened to be heavily inebriated. Forgetting his newly gained stature, he also led the stone pelting from the front. During the riot, two of his men grabbed a policeman from behind and pulled him into a deserted alley, and Velappan dropped a huge brick on the cop's head. Thankfully, the policeman shifted his weight at the last moment and escaped certain death. Naturally, the policemen responded harshly to this particular case of violence. Velappan was carried off into the police van and beaten up severely. By the time he was taken to the lock-up, he was unconscious.

When the protest turned violent, the public, who had until then supported the labourers, changed their tune.

The foundations of the protest were shaken. Eventually, by the time the labour leaders agreed to discuss and arrive at an agreeable solution without any demands, many innocent labourers were in prison. Velappan was in the deepest trouble among them. Even after the union leaders, and in turn, some ministers, tried to get him released, the cops refused to let go of someone who had almost killed one of their men. A grim shadow fell on Raani's life.

Although Chaalai Bazaar returned to its usual bustle on the festive day, Guruswamy's plantation was filled with gloom.

'Why did Velappan go that far? What's his tie with the Chaalai labour union? If he cared so much about the labourers, he could have just joined the protest and chanted a few slogans. But when has he ever practised any moderation? I heard he was fully drunk, too! Can you escape so easily after you lay hands on a policeman? Look what has happened now… Even the minister has said there's nothing he can do about it. The minister in question was once our Saami's classmate, I hear. He was very close to Saami in those days, during their involvement in the rallies for independence. But our Saami never goes to anyone for recommendations or favours… Poor Raani, she is at Saami's home all day, weeping her heart out…'

Everyone in the neighbourhood believed that Guruswamy would somehow bring Velappan out of police custody.

12

'I CAN'T, RAANI! I JUST CAN'T DO THAT. HE SHOULD FACE the consequences for what he did. I have never in my life gone to anyone asking for favours. Remember when you eloped with Velappan, how your family sent a mob of henchmen to threaten me into giving up your whereabouts? Even on that occasion, we called for the police and took care of the situation. Some people asked me to pull some strings and teach your brothers a good lesson. But I didn't. My life was in danger then, and yet, I would rather have died than seek favour from influential people.'

'Saamiyappa, who else can I go to?'

It was growing dark. Guruswamy stared ahead from his terrace, lost in a stream of thoughts. The darkness spreading from the horizon gripped the neighbourhood in a strange gloom.

Raani looked at Guruswamy expectantly. Had this good man, the pillar of her hopes, transformed completely now? Where had the compassion, humility and calmness in his voice gone?

Would she never hear the kind call – 'Raaniyammov!' – from the black-bearded, soft-eyed man any more?

'I can't, Raani! I just can't do that…' These were the only words she had repeatedly received from Guruswamy these past five days, ever since Velappan was arrested.

In those five days, she had sought refuge on Guruswamy's terrace, with her child in hand, begging him to get her husband out. And she had received only this curt response…

Saamiyappa cannot be so stone-hearted. All that fuss that my husband made at the Devi temple in his drunken state… The way he insulted Saamiyappa, who was like a god to our family… Saamiyappa was also human, after all! This is probably out of that resentment, she thought at first.

But the past five days, Guruswamy had left Raani and her child in his room and walked up and down on his terrace every night. When Raani asked if he was not sleepy, there was only an absent-minded 'Hmm?' in response from him. Had his heart turned foul in the process of him becoming handsome? Had she known, she would never have asked him to shave his beard off!

Parvathi was the only solace Raani had now.

'I have no one to turn to any more, Parvathi. Even

Saamiyappa has bluntly refused to help because of his ill feelings towards my husband. What do I do, Parvathi? I'm holding on to my life only for this child.'

'Stop fretting, Raaniyamma. Be patient. Your husband is a smart fellow. He'll be out soon. Don't beat yourself up over this,' Parvathi consoled her naively.

'What do you know, Parvathi? His smarts will be of no use in the hands of the police. What he did was such a terrible crime. This cursed drinking habit also led him astray. His drinking is to blame. His colleagues came and reported that he's beaten up severely every day. I felt half dead hearing the news. His party men tried their best but could not get bail. They say Saamiyappa can get him out if only he tried. I never imagined Saamiyappa would be so headstrong in this matter.'

Guruswamy stood at his terrace as if in severe penance. The sun was setting behind the coconut trees in the distance, and the day was drawing to a close. Raani had taken up the responsibility of lighting all the lamps in the Devi temple.

The temple yard was bright with the lights from the lamps. Some children were playfully ringing the temple bell. Vengu sang a verse praising Devi in his soulful voice. People from the neighbouring streets were gathered in the temple yard, their shadows dancing in the light thrown by the lamps. Their chatter drowned even the tolling bells. Were they all discussing the same thing? *Saami can do it if he puts his mind to it. Only Guruswamy can do it.*

'Saamiyappo, what are you doing in this darkness?' Raani asked as she came up the stairs, child in hand, and turned on the lights in Guruswamy's room. 'Take this prasadham, Saamiyappa. I can't afford to lose all hope. I lit all the lamps and said a special prayer today. This little fellow doesn't even let me pray in peace! He was crying the whole time…'

'I don't want the prasadham, Raani. I haven't even showered today…'

'Oh, that's why you didn't come down to the temple during the prayer! Even Pappan and Ravi enquired about you. What if you haven't showered? It's still our offering to Devi. Nothing wrong with it. Take it.'

'I don't need Devi's offering…'

'Saamiyappa, what is this?'

'I need your offering, Raani…'

A heavy silence settled between them. When Raani began to realize the gravity of Guruswamy's words, she felt she saw a blazing fire all around her. Fire… Ablaze… The smoke that she had so far mistaken for fog was now cleared by that blazing fire.

She went to her wailing child, comforted him and put him to sleep on the bed. Even when she proceeded to complete her tasks in the kitchen one by one, Guruswamy stood on the terrace, staring resolutely into the darkness.

How long had he stood like that?

Even when Raani turned off the lights and came to stand beside him, he remained completely still.

'Saamiyappa!'

'Saamiyappa…' she called, pulling his hands and placing them on her breasts.

Guruswamy turned to face her in a flash.

'Devi, I accept your offering now…' he thought.

Guruswamy moved his hands off her breasts and lifted her face to look into her eyes. Those dark, shiny eyes… To take a long look at her face…

'Saamiyappa, can you somehow bring him back tomorrow?'

He was jolted suddenly into a deep abyss…

'I know you can do it if you try, Saamiyappa… Bring him back somehow, Saamiyappa…'

Raani pulled him into a tight hug. She pulled his face close to her lips and whispered, 'Please bring him back somehow…'

'Raani… Let me… go…'

He pulled free from her, rushed into his room and turned on the lights.

In the sudden flood of light, Raani stood weakly like a deranged woman.

'Saamiyappa!'

'Stay here, Raani. I'll get him out somehow…' he called out in a hoarse voice, already rushing down the steps. When he crossed the temple yard and stepped onto the road, the street lay in pitch darkness.

Raani stood motionless on the terrace, staring at the large portrait of the majestic, bearded Guruswamy on the wall of the living room, as if seeing it for the first time.

ALSO AVAILABLE BY HACHETTE INDIA

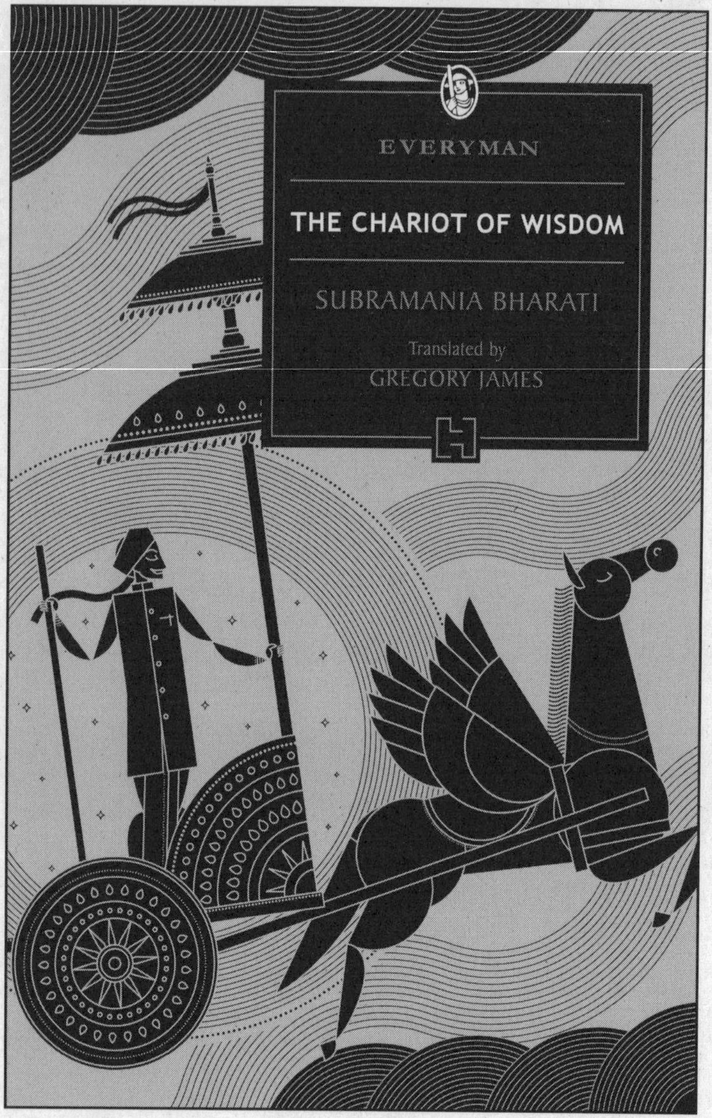

THE CHARIOT OF WISDOM

SUBRAMANIA BHARATI

Translated and with an introduction by GREGORY JAMES

SPECIAL BILINGUAL EDITION

NATIONALIZED TAMIL BOOKS IN TRANSLATION SERIES

Breaking the constraints of style and imagery central to classical Tamil literature, Mahakavi C. Subramania Bharati (1882–1921) heralded a new era for the language by making it simpler, thereby encouraging a wider readership. His prodigious contribution to the writings of his homeland – done while in exile during a tumultuous time in the nation's freedom movement – has since propelled his stature to that of a revered literary figure in the subcontinent.

In *The Chariot of Wisdom*, his only novella, a vexed journalist, plagued by material worries and the daily attrition of twentieth-century, British-occupied India, escapes into a daydream to realms mystical and unexplored. He navigates an imaginary chariot through The World of Tranquillity, The World of Pleasure, The World of Truth and The World of Dharma, and finds his values and ideals informing, competing and often contradicting one another. As his self-doubts deepen, he battles the notion that peace and happiness come at a price.

A critical examination of a colonized, afflicted civilization marred by corruption and greed, Bharati's pioneering work speaks to a morally wounded country through astute observations and lively humour. Translated with refined intellectual acuity by Gregory James, this modern classic – as timely today as it was a century ago – is a cleverly masked plea to the people of a distracted nation to rally together in pursuit of a just society.

ALSO AVAILABLE BY HACHETTE INDIA

THE SOUND OF WAVES

'KALKI' R. KRISHNAMURTHY
Translated by GOWRI RAMNARAYAN

NATIONALIZED TAMIL BOOKS IN TRANSLATION SERIES

WINNER OF THE FICCI BOOK OF THE YEAR (2023) – BEST TRANSLATION SPECIAL JURY AWARD

A fractured country on the verge of freedom finds its people navigating the slippery crevices of love, morality and nationalism.

To escape the despair of his all-consuming, failed relationship with Dharini, Raghavan agrees to meet Lalita in an arranged match. Finding Lalita's cousin, the vivacious and captivating Sita, a far more amenable fit, he marries her instead. With a charming wife and a powerful government job in pre-Partition Delhi adding to his smug contentment, Raghavan turns a blind eye to the evils of the British Raj. Along comes Sita's cousin Surya, a dauntless revolutionary burning to right all wrongs. His commitment to the socialist credo leads him to Dharini, a young and spirited party member, the woman Raghavan continues to long for. Cracks appear in the brittle foundations of their lives as the characters move across rural Thanjavur, Madras, Bombay, Karachi, New Delhi, Agra, Calcutta and Lahore.

With poignant detail and lyrical prose, Kalki's tour de force lays bare the emotions of ordinary people grappling with extraordinary changes, their circumstances riven with misfortunes, disasters and the carnage of Partition. *The Sound of Waves* is an impassioned tribute to everyday citizens and their woes, and an acute commentary on the aspirations of an emerging nation.

This book by Gowri Ramnarayan is the English translation of the bestselling Tamil novel *Alai Osai* by freedom fighter and novelist 'Kalki' R. Krishnamurthy (1899–1954).

KURINJI MALAR

NA. PARTHASARATHY

Translated by MALINI SESHADRI

NATIONALIZED TAMIL BOOKS IN TRANSLATION SERIES

On a rock on the road to a hill temple are carved the names 'Aravindan' and 'Poorani'.

Barely out of her teens, Poorani is plunged into crisis with the sudden passing of her father. As she brings her life back on course, fate arranges a meeting with Aravindan. Gentle and idealistic, Aravindan makes it his goal to right the wrongs in society. Spirited and refined, Poorani blazes a trail to recognition and renown with her public-speaking knowhow. Their friendship soon blossoms into love. But can a world riddled with opportunism and deceit ever hold their dreams and ideals?

Written more than six decades ago and set in Madurai and the surrounding areas of the Tamil land, this classic romance – peopled by an array of compelling characters – was first serialized in a magazine in the 1960s, and later attained further popularity on-screen. Believed to be Na. Parthasarathy's magnum opus, *Kurinji Malar* is a sweeping saga that conjures an unforgettable landscape of hope and heartbreak – a delicate balance only a master storyteller can offer.

ALSO AVAILABLE BY HACHETTE INDIA

CASTE AWAY: PERSPECTIVES ON CASTE-EQUALITY STRUGGLES IN TAMIL NADU

NA. VANAMAMALAI

Translated and with an introduction by JOSHUA GNANASELVAN

NATIONALIZED TAMIL BOOKS IN TRANSLATION SERIES

A pithy and momentous collection of essays on caste-equality struggles in Tamil Nadu by scholar and social activist Na. Vanamamalai

Offering a meticulous exploration of Tamil Nadu's intricate caste dynamics, Na. Vanamamalai's pivotal work unveils the endeavours of 'lower-caste' communities in challenging established hierarchies. It spans the Chola dynasty to the early part of the twentieth century. Through extensive research and insightful analysis, the renowned scholar elucidates how certain communities strategically appropriated the *varna* system, elevating their social status. Drawing on various source texts – historical documents, verses by socially committed ascetics, court judgments – the work demonstrates how the Chola kings tactically offered concessions to different caste clusters, thereby navigating a delicate balance between benefits and exploitation.

Caste Away compellingly argues that caste-based conflicts were fundamentally manifestations of class antagonisms, and challenges conventional interpretations, showing how the pursuit of caste equality was aimed not at creating an egalitarian society but at elevating the social standing of specific castes.

TAMIL HEROIC POETRY

K. KAILASAPATHY

Foreword by A.R. VENKATACHALAPATHY

An elegant and thorough examination of the riches of Sangam poetry

In this acclaimed comparative study, K. Kailasapathy, the celebrated Sri Lankan academic and critic, introduces and interprets ancient Tamil poems and examines the stylistic heritage, themes and motifs pervading Sangam poetry while building the literary corpus's bridge to heroic poetry in other languages – most notably Greek. He identifies the formulaic expression, stock phrases and overarching sensibilities pervasive in the poems and, going much against the popular grain, expands on the notion that oral verse-making is central to Sangam poetry.

A nod to Milman Parry, this deeply necessary exploration of our neglected past is an engaging and accessible discourse on one of our most fertile literary ages and, with much agility, connects the dots in studying early Tamil poetry for a modern reader.